HARL...
Pre...

With Valentine's Day, February is always a romantic month. And we've got some great books in store for you....

The High-Society Wife by Helen Bianchin is the story of a marriage of convenience between two rich and powerful families.... But what this couple didn't expect is for their marriage to become real! It's also the first in our new miniseries RUTHLESS, where you'll find commanding men, who stop at nothing to get what they want. Look out for more books coming soon! And if you love Italian men, don't miss *The Marchese's Love-Child* by Sara Craven, where our heroine is swept off her feet by a passionate tycoon.

If you just want to get away from it all, let us whisk you off to the beautiful Greek Islands in Julia James's hard-hitting story *Baby of Shame*. What will happen when a businessman discovers that his night of passion with a young Englishwoman five years ago resulted in a son? The Caribbean is the destination for our couple in Anne Mather's intriguing tale *The Virgin's Seduction*.

Jane Porter has a dangerously sexy Sicilian for you in *The Sicilian's Defiant Mistress*. This explosive reunion story promises to be dark and passionate! In Trish Morey's *Stolen by the Sheikh*, the first in her new duet, THE ARRANGED BRIDES, a young woman is summoned to the palace of a demanding sheikh, who has plans for her future.... Don't miss part two, coming in March.

See the inside front cover for a list of titles and book numbers.

FOREIGN AFFAIRS

Surrender to seduction under a golden sun.

Why not relax and let a Harlequin Presents®
book whisk you away to stunning international
locations, where irresistible men and
sophisticated women fall in love....

Don't miss this opportunity to experience
glamorous lifestyles and exotic settings in

The Virgin's Seduction
by Anne Mather

A world full of passion...

Coming in May 2006
The Italian's Price
by Diana Hamilton
#2539

Anne Mather

THE VIRGIN'S SEDUCTION

F REIGN

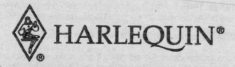

HARLEQUIN®

TORONTO • NEW YORK • LONDON
AMSTERDAM • PARIS • SYDNEY • HAMBURG
STOCKHOLM • ATHENS • TOKYO • MILAN • MADRID
PRAGUE • WARSAW • BUDAPEST • AUCKLAND

If you purchased this book without a cover you should be aware that this book is stolen property. It was reported as "unsold and destroyed" to the publisher, and neither the author nor the publisher has received any payment for this "stripped book."

ISBN 0-373-12519-4

THE VIRGIN'S SEDUCTION

First North American Publication 2006.

Copyright © 2005 by Anne Mather.

All rights reserved. Except for use in any review, the reproduction or utilization of this work in whole or in part in any form by any electronic, mechanical or other means, now known or hereafter invented, including xerography, photocopying and recording, or in any information storage or retrieval system, is forbidden without the written permission of the publisher, Harlequin Enterprises Limited, 225 Duncan Mill Road, Don Mills, Ontario, Canada M3B 3K9.

All characters in this book have no existence outside the imagination of the author and have no relation whatsoever to anyone bearing the same name or names. They are not even distantly inspired by any individual known or unknown to the author, and all incidents are pure invention.

This edition published by arrangement with Harlequin Books S.A.

® and TM are trademarks of the publisher. Trademarks indicated with ® are registered in the United States Patent and Trademark Office, the Canadian Trade Marks Office and in other countries.

www.eHarlequin.com

Printed in U.S.A.

All about the author...
Anne Mather

I've always wanted to write—which is not to say I've always wanted to be a professional writer. For years I wrote only for my own pleasure, and it wasn't until my husband suggested that I ought to send one of my stories to a publisher that we put several publishers' names into a hat and pulled one out. The rest, as they say, is history. And now, more than 150 books later, I'm literally—excuse the pun—staggered by what happened.

I had written all through my childhood and into my teens; the stories changing from children's adventures to torrid gypsy passions. My mother used to gather these up from time to time, when my bedroom became too untidy, and dispose of them! The trouble was, I never used to finish any of the stories, and *Caroline,* my first published book, was the first book I'd actually completed. I was newly married then, and my daughter was just a baby, and it was quite a job juggling my household chores and scribbling away in exercise books every chance I got. Not very professional, as you can see, but that's the way it was.

I now have two grown-up children, a son and daughter, and two adorable grandchildren, Abigail and Ben. My e-mail address is mystic-am@msn.com and I'd be happy to hear from any of my readers.

CHAPTER ONE

ELLIE came to find her as Eve was shovelling manure out of Storm's stall. The work should have been done that morning, but Mick hadn't turned in today and Eve had offered to help out.

Nevertheless, Eve felt a little self-conscious when the old lady raised her handkerchief to her nose before saying, 'Come outside. I want to talk to you.'

Eve didn't argue. You didn't argue with her grandmother, and the old lady's cane tap-tapped its way back along the aisle between the row of empty stalls. Meanwhile, Eve jammed the fork she was using into her wheelbarrow and, after checking to see that she had no dirt on her hands, followed Ellie out into the crisp evening air.

It was November, and the scent of woodsmoke banished the smell of the stables. Already there was a tracing of frost on the trees in the copse, and the lights that surrounded the stable yard had a sparkling brilliance.

'Cassie's coming tomorrow.'

The old lady waited only long enough for Eve to emerge from the doorway before making her blunt announcement, and her granddaughter's stomach tightened. But she knew better than to show any obvious reaction, and with a shrug of her thin shoulders she said, 'Don't you mean Cassandra?'

'No, I mean Cassie,' retorted the old lady shortly, wrapping the woollen pashmina she was wearing over her tweed jacket tighter about her ample form. 'I christened my daughter Cassie, not Cassandra. If she wants to call herself by that damn fool name, I don't have to follow suit.'

Eve acknowledged this with a wry arching of her dark brows, but she thought it was significant that Ellie was wearing the wrap Cassie had given her several years ago. Was this a sign that she'd forgiven her daughter at last? That the rapidly approaching demands of old age had reminded her that her time was slipping away?

'How long is she coming for?' asked Eve casually, aware that, whatever Ellie said, this was not going to be an easy time for any of them. She and Cassandra could never be friends, and it might be easier all round if she simply moved into a hotel for a couple of weeks.

'She didn't say.' Ellie's tone was grumpy. 'As usual, I'm supposed to accommodate myself to her needs. Oh, and by the way, she's bringing some man with her. I don't know who he is, but knowing Cassie he's probably someone who can help her with her career.'

'Oh, well…' Eve tried to sound philosophical. 'If she's bringing a boyfriend I doubt if she'll be staying long. He must have commitments; a business, maybe.' She tugged her lower lip between her teeth. 'What do you want me to do?'

Ellie's eyes, which were extraordinarily like her granddaughter's, narrowed in surprise. 'Why should I want you to do anything?' She gave a shiver as the wind, which had a decidedly northerly bite to it, whistled across the stable yard. 'I just thought I ought to—to—'

'Warn me?'

'To *tell* you,' she insisted tersely. 'If I could put her off, I would.'

'No, you wouldn't.' Eve's tone was dry. She wasn't taken in by her grandmother's last remark. 'You're really delighted she's coming to see you, even if she is using this place as her own private hotel. As usual.'

'Eve—'

'Look, I understand where you're coming from, Ellie. I do. So—would you like me to find somewhere else to stay while she's here? I'm sure Harry—'

'We'll leave the Reverend Murray's name out of this.' The old lady looked scandalised at her suggestion. 'You can't stay with him. It wouldn't be seemly. In any case, this is your home. I don't want you to move out.'

'Okay.'

Eve was dismissive, but the old lady wasn't finished. 'This is Northumberland,' she said, with a quaver to her voice. 'Not north London. You're not living in some smelly squat now.'

That was a low blow, but it was a sign that her grandmother wasn't as blasé about Cassie's visit as she pretended. Ellie seldom if ever mentioned where Eve had been living when Ellie had arrived to rescue her, and she could see from the old lady's expression that she already regretted speaking so bluntly. But Ellie must remember that the last time Cassie was here she and Eve had barely said a word to one another.

As if needing some reassurance, she added, 'Are you saying you don't want to be here while Cassie's staying?' All the ambivalence she was feeling about the visit showed in her lined, anxious face. 'Because if you are—'

'I just thought it might be easier all round if I left you to it,' Eve muttered unwillingly. She didn't want to hurt the woman who was her closest relative and her friend.

'Well, it isn't,' declared her grandmother, pushing the hand that wasn't holding her cane into her pocket for warmth. 'So we'll say no more about Henry Murray. And it's too cold to stand here gossiping, anyway. We'll talk about this again later. Over supper, perhaps.'

But they wouldn't, Eve knew. Her grandmother had spoken, and in her own way she was just as selfish as Cassie. Oh, she would never have abandoned her child at birth, or ignored its existence for the first fifteen years of its life. But she liked her own way, and Eve rarely felt strongly enough about anything to argue with her.

'You'll be in soon, won't you?' Ellie asked now, and Eve nodded.

'As soon as I've got Storm back in his stall,' she promised.

'Good.'

Her grandmother looked as if she would have liked to say something more, but thought better of it. With a farewell lift of her cane, she trudged away towards the lights of the house.

The hired Aston Martin ate up the miles between London and the north of England. Jake liked motorway driving, mostly because the journey—this journey—would be over that much quicker. He hadn't wanted to come, and the sooner this trip was over the better he'd like it.

'Shall we stop and have some lunch?'

Cassandra was being determinedly cheerful, but for once he didn't respond to her lively chatter. This was wrong, he thought. He shouldn't be here. Bringing him to meet her mother smacked of a relationship they simply didn't have.

Oh, they'd been spending time together, off and on, for the past six months, but it wasn't serious. Well, in his case it wasn't, anyway. He had no intention of marrying again. Or of setting up home with someone like Cassandra, he conceded ruefully. He liked her company now and then, but he knew that living with her would drive him up the wall.

'Did you hear what I said, darling?'

Cassandra was determined to have an answer, and Jake turned his head to give her a fleeting look. 'I heard,' he said. 'But there's nowhere to eat around here.'

'There's a service area coming up,' protested his companion. 'There, you see: it's only another five miles.'

'I'm not in the mood for soggy fries and burgers,' Jake told her drily. He glanced at the thin gold watch circling his wrist. 'It's only a quarter of one. We should be there in less than an hour.'

'I doubt it.'

Cassandra was sulky, and once again Jake permitted himself a glance in her direction. 'You did say it was only a couple hundred miles,' he reminded her. 'As I see it, we've covered at least three-quarters of the journey already.'

Cassandra gave a careless shrug. 'I may have underestimated a little.'

Jake's fingers tightened on the wheel. 'Did you?'

'Well, yes.' Cassandra turned towards him now, all eager for his forgiveness. 'But I knew you'd never agree if I told you it was over three hundred miles from London.'

Her fingers slipped over the sleeve of his sweater, seeking the point where the fine black wool gave way to lean, darkly tanned flesh. The tips of her fingers feathered over the dark hairs that escaped the cuff of his sweater, but he didn't respond to the intimacy of her touch. Three hundred miles, he was thinking. That meant they had at least a couple of hours to go. It also meant they would have to stop somewhere for Cassandra to toy with a salad and sip a skinny latte. Although she rarely ate a proper meal, she insisted on drinking numerous cups of coffee every chance she got.

'You do forgive me, don't you, darling?' She had nestled closer now and, in spite of the obstacle the centre console presented, she laid her head on his shoulder. 'So—can we stop soon? I'm dying for the loo.'

Faced with that request, Jake knew he didn't have any option, and although he didn't say anything he indicated left and pulled off the motorway into the service area she'd pointed out. It was busy. Even in November, people were always going somewhere, and Jake had to park at the far side of the ground. He just hoped the car would still be there when they came back.

'This is fun, isn't it?' Cassandra said, after they had served themselves and occupied a table for two by the window. As usual, she'd helped herself to a salad, carefully avoiding all the mayonnaise-covered options and sticking to lettuce, tomato and peppers. She sipped at the bottled water she'd had to choose when no skinny latte was available. 'It gives us a bit more time on our own.'

'We could have spent time alone if we'd stayed in town,' Jake reminded her flatly. He parted the two slices of his sandwich to discover the almost transparent piece of ham covering the bread. When would the British learn that a ham sandwich needed a proper filling? he wondered gloomily, as a wave of nostalgia for his homeland swept over him. What he wouldn't give to be back in the Caribbean right now.

'I know,' Cassandra said, reaching across the table to cover his hand with hers. Long scarlet nails dug into the skin of his wrist. 'But we'll have some fun, I promise.'

Jake doubted that. From what Cassandra had told him, her mother was already well into her seventies. Cassandra had been a late baby, she'd explained, and her brother,

her only sibling, was at least fifteen years older than she was.

Jake wasn't absolutely sure how old Cassandra was. In her late thirties, he imagined, which made her half a dozen years older than he was, though that had never been a problem. Besides, in television or theatre age was always a moot point. Actresses were as old as they appeared, and some of them got *ingénue* roles well into their forties.

'So, tell me about Watersmeet,' he said, trying to be positive. 'Who lives there besides your mother? You said it's quite a large property. I imagine she has people who work for her, doesn't she?'

'Oh...' Cassandra drew her full lips together. 'Well, there's Mrs Blackwood. She's Mummy's housekeeper. And old Bill Trivett. He looks after the garden and grounds. We used to have several stable hands when Mummy bred horses, but now all the animals have been sold, so I imagine they're not needed any more.'

Jake frowned. 'Don't you know?'

Cassandra's pale, delicate features took on a little colour. 'It—it has been some time since I've been home,' she said defensively. Then, seeing his expression, she hurried on, 'I have been busy, darling. And, as you're finding out, Northumberland is not the easiest place to get to.'

'There are planes,' Jake commented, taking a bite out of his sandwich, relieved to find that at least the bread was fresh.

'Air fares are expensive,' insisted Cassandra, not altogether truthfully. 'And I wouldn't like to scrounge from my mother.'

'If you say so.'

Jake wasn't prepared to argue with her, particularly about something that wasn't his problem. If she chose to neglect her mother, that was her affair.

'Doesn't Mrs Wilkes have a companion?' he asked now, his mind running on the old lady's apparent isolation, and once again he saw the colour come and go in Cassandra's face.

'Well, there's Eve,' she said reluctantly, without elaborating. 'And my mother's surname is Robertson, not Wilkes.'

'Really?'

Jake regarded her enquiringly, and with evident unwillingness she was obliged to explain. 'I changed my name when I moved to London,' she said tersely. 'Lots of actors do the same.'

'Mmm.' Jake accepted this. But then, because he was intrigued by her apparent reticence, he added, 'And what about Eve? Is she some elderly contemporary of your mother's?' Faint amusement touched the corners of his thin mouth. 'Doesn't she approve of you, or what?'

'Heavens, no!' Cassandra spoke irritably now, and he wondered what he'd said to arouse this reaction. 'Eve is— a distant relative, that's all. Mummy brought her to live with her—oh, perhaps ten years ago.'

'As a companion?'

'Partly.' Cassandra huffed. 'She actually works as an infant teacher at the village school.'

Jake made no response to this, but he absorbed both what she'd told him and what she hadn't. It seemed from his observations that Cassandra resented this woman's presence in her home. Perhaps she was jealous of the relationship she had with Cassandra's mother. Possibly the woman was younger, too, though that was less certain. Whatever, Jake would welcome her existence. At least there would be someone else to dilute the ambivalence of his own situation.

They reached the village of Falconbridge in the late

afternoon. The traffic on the Newcastle by-pass had been horrendous, due to an accident between a car and a wagon. Luckily it appeared that no one had been hurt, but it had reduced the carriageway to one lane in their direction.

The last few miles of the journey had been through the rolling countryside of Redesdale, with the Cheviot Hills in the distance turning a dusky purple in the fading light. Despite his misgivings about the trip, Jake had to admit the place had a certain mystery about it, and he could quite believe Roman legions still stalked these hills after dark.

A latent interest in his surroundings was sparked, and he felt a twinge of impatience when Cassandra shivered and hugged herself as if she was cold. 'This place,' she muttered. 'I can't imagine why anyone would want to stay here. Give me bright lights and civilised living every time.'

'I think it's beautiful,' said Jake, slowing to negotiate one of the blind summits that were a frequent hazard of the road. 'I know a lot of people who live in London who would love to leave the rat race and come here. Only not everyone has the luxury of such an escape.'

Cassandra cast him a disbelieving look. 'You're not trying to tell me that you'd prefer to live here instead of San Felipe?'

'No.' Jake was honest. Much as he liked to travel, there was nowhere quite as appealing as his island home. 'But I was talking about London,' he reminded her. 'You have to admit, there are too many people in too small a space.'

'Well, I like it.' Cassandra wasn't persuaded. 'When you work in the media, as I do, you need to be at the heart of things.'

'Yeah.'

Jake conceded the point, but in the six months since he'd known her Cassandra had only had one acting role that he knew of. And then it had only been an advertisement for some new face cream, though she'd told him that advertising work certainly helped to pay the bills.

They approached the village over an old stone structure spanning a rushing stream. The original Falcon Bridge, he concluded, glad they hadn't encountered another vehicle on its narrow pass. Beyond, a row of grey stone cottages edged the village street, lights glinting from windows, smoke curling from chimneys into the crisp evening air.

'My mother's house is on the outskirts of the village,' Cassandra said, realising she would have to give him directions. 'Just follow the road through and you'll see it. It's set back, behind some trees.'

'Set back' was something of an understatement, Jake found. Turning between stone gateposts, they drove over a quarter of a mile before reaching the house itself. Banks of glossy rhododendrons reared at one side of the drive, while tall poplars, bare and skeletal in the half-light, lined the other.

Watersmeet looked solid and substantial. Like the cottages in the village, it was built of stone, with three floors and gables at every corner. There were tall windows on the ground floor, flanking a centre doorway, uncurtained at present and spilling golden light onto the gravelled forecourt.

'Well, we're here,' said Cassandra unnecessarily, making no attempt to get out of the car. She gathered the sides of her fake fur jacket, wrapping it closely about her. 'I wonder if they know we're here?'

'There's one way to find out,' remarked Jake, pushing open his door and swinging his long legs over the sill. He instantly felt the cold, and reached into the back to rescue his leather jacket. Then, pushing his arms into the sleeves, he got to his feet.

The front door opened as he buttoned the jacket, and a woman appeared, silhouetted by the glowing light from the hall behind her. She was tall and slim, that much he could see, with what appeared to be a rope of dark hair hanging over one shoulder.

Obviously not Cassandra's mother, he realised, even as he heard Cassandra utter an impatient oath. The distant relative? he wondered. Surely she wasn't old enough to be the housekeeper Cassandra had mentioned?

The protesting sound as the car door was thrust back on its hinges distracted him. Turning his head, he saw Cassandra pulling herself to her feet and, unlike the other woman's, her face was clearly visible.

'Eve,' she said, unknowingly answering his question, her thin smile and tightly controlled features an indication that he hadn't been mistaken about her hostility towards this woman. 'Where's my mother? I thought she'd have come to meet us.'

The girl—for he could see now that she was little more—came down the three shallow steps towards them. And as she moved into the light cast by the uncurtained windows Jake saw her pale olive-skinned features were much like his own. He guessed her eyes would be dark, too, though he couldn't see them. She barely looked at him, however, her whole attention focussed on Cassandra, but he saw she had a warm, exotic kind of beauty, and he wondered why she was content to apparently spend her days looking after an old woman, distant relative or not.

Her mouth compressed for a moment before she spoke. Was it his imagination or was she as unenthusiastic to see Cassandra as she was to see her? 'I'm afraid Ellie's in bed,' she said, without offering a greeting. 'She had a fall yesterday evening and Dr McGuire thinks she might have broken one of the bones in her ankle.'

'Might have?' Cassandra fastened onto the words. 'Why is there any doubt about it? Shouldn't she have had her ankle X-rayed or something?'

'She should,' agreed Eve, and Jake noticed that she didn't let Cassandra's agitation get to her. 'But she wanted to be here when you arrived, and if she'd had to go to the hospital in Newcastle...' She shrugged. 'I've arranged for an ambulance to take her in tomorrow—'

'An ambulance!' Cassandra snorted. 'Why couldn't you take her?'

Eve's face was a cool mask. 'I have a job to do,' she replied flatly. And now she looked at Jake fully for the first time. 'Would you—both—like to come in?'

CHAPTER TWO

AN HOUR later, Eve was able to escape to her room to change for supper.

She'd spent the time between the guests' arrival and now escorting Cassie to see her mother, showing Jacob Romero to his room—Ellie had been adamant that Cassie shouldn't sleep with her lover under *her* roof—and arranging with Mrs Blackwood for refreshments to be provided in the library.

Eve, herself, had done her best to keep out of Cassie's way after she'd delivered her to her mother. Out of Jacob Romero's way, too, with his deepset eyes and dark, attractive features. She didn't know what she'd expected Cassie's escort to be like. She only knew she couldn't call him her *boy*friend. There was nothing remotely boyish about Jacob Romero, and from the moment she'd seen him standing beside his car in the courtyard she'd felt a curious sense of foreboding that she couldn't quite place.

She supposed she'd been expecting someone older. Cassie was forty-six, after all. But Romero was obviously much younger. Tall—he was easily six feet and more—with a well-muscled chest and a flat stomach tapering to narrow hips, he looked strong and virile. An impression increased by his hair, which was cut very close to his head.

He looked—dangerous, she thought. Dangerously attractive, at least. And sexy—a description that in his case wasn't exaggerated. It was easy to understand what Cassie

19

saw in him. What troubled Eve most was that she could see it, too.

She pulled a face at her reflection in the mirror of her dressing table. Then, shedding her shirt and jeans onto the floor, she went to take her shower. She was being fanciful, she thought. Ten years ago, feeling a man's eyes upon her wouldn't have bothered her so much. But she'd been harder then, wary and streetwise. In the years since she'd come to live with her grandmother she'd become softer. She'd let down the guard she'd had since she was old enough to understand.

Drying her hair later, she mentally ran through the contents of her wardrobe. Nothing very exciting there, she acknowledged. Skirts and blouses or sweaters for school; jeans and sweaters for home. For the rare occasions when she went out her grandmother had bought her a little black velvet dress, with long sleeves, a scoop neckline, and a skirt that skimmed her kneecaps. But this was not that kind of occasion, and she had no intention of attracting Cassie's curiosity by wearing something totally unsuitable for the evening meal.

She was tempted to leave her hair loose, something she often did in the evenings after she'd washed it. But once again she decided against drawing attention to herself. She plaited the glossy black strands into the usual single braid, securing it with a narrow band of elasticated ribbon.

After far too much deliberation, she put on a V-necked top made of elasticised cotton. Bands of ivory ribbon hid the shaping both around her arms and above and below her breasts, contrasting with the rest of the garment, whose jade-green colour complemented her pale skin.

She almost took it off again when she saw how well it suited her. She'd bought the top on one of her infrequent trips to Newcastle, and had pushed it away in a drawer because she'd thought it was unsuitable for school. Now, looking at it again, she saw she'd been right. It was more in keeping with the teenage girl her grandmother had found subsisting in a draughty squat.

But it was too late to be having second thoughts now. Besides, she doubted she'd be eating with her grandmother's guests. She had no intention of leaving the old lady to eat alone, or of playing gooseberry to Cassie's tête-à-tête.

Zipping on a pair of black cords, she paused only long enough to stroke her lids with a dark brown shadow and run a peachy gloss over her mouth. Then, slipping her feet into heelless mules, she left her room before she could change her mind.

Watersmeet was a fairly large house, but over the years Eve had got used to it, and now she hardly noticed its high-ceilinged rooms and wide corridors. Some years before she'd come to live here central heating had been installed, but the boiler struggled to keep the place at an ambient temperature. Consequently, at this time of year, fires were lit in all the downstairs rooms that were used.

Eve went first to the kitchen, to see how Mrs Blackwood was coping. The elderly housekeeper wasn't used to having guests, but very little fazed her. At present, she was rolling curls of homemade cream cheese in slices of ham, and an avocado dressing waited to be served in tiny ramekins to accompany each plate.

'Her Ladyship won't eat any of the dressing,' Mrs Blackwood explained, when Eve commented on the arrangement. The woman meant Cassie, she knew. Her grandmother didn't watch the calories these days. 'Just hope she approves of the sea bass,' she continued. 'I asked Mr Goddard to deliver it specially. I know how fussy she is about eating meat.'

Eve smiled. 'I'm sure it will be a delicious meal,' she said warmly. 'What have we got for dessert?'

'Bread and butter pudding and ice cream,' said Mrs Blackwood at once. 'I know it's fattening, but it is Mrs Robertson's favourite. I thought she deserved something really nice, after having that fall and all.'

'Mmm.' Eve nodded appreciatively. Mrs Blackwood's bread and butter pudding, which she made with brioche and peaches, was famous in the village. She usually contributed individual puddings whenever the church had a coffee morning, and it always sold out at summer bakes and Christmas fairs.

'You think your grandmother will approve, then?'

'I think she'll be delighted,' Eve assured her. 'Which reminds me, I'd better go and see how she is. I hope nothing's been said to upset her.'

'I shouldn't worry.' Mrs Blackwood looked up from her task as she made for the door. 'Your grandmother's a tough old bird, Eve. She's had to be, if you get my meaning. I'm not saying she doesn't love her daughter. Of course she does. But she's known her too long to be upset by anything Cassie says.'

'I hope you're right.'

Eve let herself out of the door and headed for the stairs. The large entrance hall of the building struck her as chilly, after the cosy warmth of the kitchen, and she wondered if she ought to fetch a sweater while she was upstairs. But then, as she put her foot on the bottom stair, she realised someone was coming down. Looking up, she saw Jacob Romero descending towards her, and that thought went out of her head.

He'd changed his clothes, too, she noticed, though she quickly dropped her gaze and stood back to let him pass before starting up. Evidently Cassie had warned him that they didn't dress formally for supper, but his fine wool camel-coloured sweater and black moleskin pants would have looked good in any company.

She supposed it was because they were expensive. Everything about him breathed money, which was par for the course as far as Cassie was concerned. Not that his dark good looks wouldn't have played a part. Eve had seen from the way the other woman looked at him that she very much coveted his body as well.

She'd expected him to perhaps offer a smile and go on, but he didn't. Instead, he stopped beside her, and she was instantly aware of his height. A tall girl herself she found she was usually on eye-level terms with the men she met, but Jacob Romero was several inches above her.

He was also much closer than she could have wished, and she had to steel herself not to step back from him. Was there a trace of cruel humour in the dark eyes? Was he as aware as she was of the effect he had upon her?

'I just wanted to thank you for having me here,' he said, the faint trace of some accent evident in his husky voice. Was he an American? If so, the intonation was very soft. Whatever, it only added to the sensual appeal of the man, and Eve couldn't prevent a shiver of apprehension from sliding down her spine.

'It's not my house,' she said quickly, aware that her tone had been much sharper than his. But, dammit, he disconcerted her, and she was pretty sure he knew it.

'You live here,' he murmured simply. 'Cassandra says you teach in the village. Is that an interesting occupation?'

'It's a job,' Eve responded, putting a hand firmly on the banister, making it fairly clear that as far as she was concerned the conversation was over.

He didn't take the hint. 'So—do you like living here?' he asked. 'It seems very—remote.'

'Far from civilisation, you mean?' she countered, aware
that she was being unnecessarily blunt, but unable to help
herself. He probably thought she was graceless as well as
ignorant, she reflected. It wasn't his fault that Cassie was
such a bitch.

'I meant it can't be easy having only an elderly lady
as a companion,' he amended drily. Then, with a glint of
humour tugging at his thin mouth, he added, 'Who am I
kidding? You obviously don't want us here.'

'I never said that.' Eve was appalled that she'd betrayed
her feelings so candidly. 'Naturally, Cassie's always welcome. This is her home.'

'Yeah, right.' He grinned at her discomfort, white teeth
contrasting sharply with the dark tan of his skin. 'But it's
not my home. I know.'

'That's not what I meant.' Eve had been staring at him,
but now she dropped her gaze. 'You're deliberately mis-
understanding me,' she said, concentrating her gaze some
way below the shadow of beard already showing on his
jawline. But the tight-fitting pants were just as disturbing
to her present frame of mind, the velvet-soft fabric clinging lovingly to every line and angle of the bulge between
his legs.

Dear God!

'I'm trying not to,' he said then, and his husky drawl
scraped like raw silk across her sensitised flesh. He was
much too close, much too male, and it was an effort to
remember where she'd been going before this encounter.

'I—I have to go,' she declared hurriedly, attempting to
move past him. 'Um—Mrs Robertson will be wondering
where I am.'

'The old lady?' As her breasts came up against the arm
he'd put out to stop her, she recoiled in panic. But all he

said was, 'She's not in her room. Cassandra said she in-sisted on coming downstairs to eat with us.'

Eve gathered her wits about her. The knowledge that Cassie had persuaded her mother to leave her bed, when she really needed her rest, just to join her and her para-mour for supper was bad enough. But what had just hap-pened had added a tension she really didn't need.

Yet what *had* happened? she chided herself. It had ob-viously meant less than nothing to him. And was she so afraid of male attention that having her boobs accidentally crushed against his arm turned into a major event?

Once, she wouldn't have considered it. Once, she would have fought off any attempt to get close to her, and any man who'd tried would have been nursing an aching groin for his trouble.

She was getting soft, she thought, aware that he was watching her with a strangely speculative look on his dark face. But, dammit, her nipples were still taut and tingling, and the unexpected contact with his body had caused a disturbing explosion of heat inside her.

Shaking her head, as if the simple action would clear her confusion, she said stiffly, 'Where is she? My—Mrs Robertson, I mean.'

'*Your* Mrs Robertson is in the library,' Jacob Romero told her consideringly, and she guessed her slip of the tongue had not gone unnoticed. His brows drew together above his straight, almost aquiline nose. 'Are you all right?'

Eve did step back then. This had gone far enough. 'Why wouldn't I be?' she exclaimed, managing to sound surprised at the question. She smoothed her palms, which were unusually damp, down the seams of her cords. 'If you'll excuse me, I'll go and see if she needs anything.'

If she'd thought to escape him, she was disappointed.

He accompanied her across the circular Persian carpet that occupied a prominent position in the centre of the floor. Double doors opposite opened into the library, which had been her grandfather's study while he was alive, but now served as both estate office and sitting room.

It was a cosy room, the books lining the walls scenting the air with the smell of old leather. A fire was burning in the large grate and Eve's grandmother was seated in her armchair beside it. A footstool supported her injured ankle, and although Eve thought she looked tired, she was defiantly holding a glass of red wine in her hand.

Cassie was there, too, occupying the chair opposite. In thin silk trousers and a matching sapphire-blue tunic, she looked blonde and elegant. Someone had dragged her grandfather's old captain's chair over from behind the desk in the corner, and it was pulled strategically close to Cassie's; obviously with Jacob Romero in mind, thought Eve cynically. Which meant she was obliged to sit on the ladder-backed dining chair that Mr Trivett used when he came to discuss estate matters.

'Help yourself to some wine, my dear,' Ellie suggested when Eve made to sit down, but Jacob Romero intervened. 'I'll get it for you,' he said, indicating the chair beside Cassie. 'And sit here. My bones are more liberally covered than yours.'

Eve doubted that. There wasn't an ounce of spare flesh on his body. And although she wanted to demur, it would have seemed uncharitable to do so. 'Thanks,' she said, and ignoring the irritation she could feel emanating from the woman beside her, she turned to Ellie. 'How are you feeling?'

'I'm feeling much better this evening,' Ellie declared, despite the fact that her usually ruddy cheeks were pale.

'Don't look so disapproving, Eve. I didn't struggle down the stairs on my own. Mr Romero carried me.'

Eve only just stopped herself from giving him an admiring look. Her grandmother was no lightweight, and he had to be fit if he'd carried the old lady down from her room.

'Um—that was good of—of you,' she murmured lamely, accepting the glass of wine he'd brought her, but she was aware that Cassie was now preening herself in his reflected glory.

'Jake's immensely strong,' she said, her smile towards him warm and intimate. Her tongue circled her upper lip in a deliberately sensual gesture as he seated himself beside Ellie. 'I suppose it's because he gets plenty of exercise.'

The *double entendre* was unmistakable, but the object of her insinuation didn't respond in kind. 'My family owns a charter company in San Felipe,' he offered smoothly, leaning forward, his arms along his thighs. His thumbs circled the glass he'd brought for himself. 'I've been hauling masts and rigging sails since I was a kid, so lifting a lightweight like you, Mrs Robertson, was no problem.'

Ellie looked pleased. 'San Felipe?' she murmured, echoing the name as Eve absorbed the fact that he wasn't an American after all. 'Is that in Spain?'

'It's an island in the Caribbean, ma'am,' he said, and Eve had an immediate image of white sands, blue seas and palm trees. No wonder he was so darkly tanned. She guessed he must be brown all over.

Now, where had that come from?

'Jake's family own the island, Mummy,' Cassie put in smugly. 'His father's retired, of course, and Jake runs the company himself.'

'How nice.' Eve was pleased to see her grandmother wasn't overawed by this intimation of unlimited wealth. 'So what are you doing in England, Mr Romero? I'd have thought this was the time of year when most people visit the Caribbean.'

'It is, of course.' He sounded regretful. 'However, I'm obliged to spend at least part of the year in Europe.'

'Jake has business interests all over the world.' Cassie was evidently determined to impress her mother. 'We met last year at the Paris Boat Show—didn't we, darling?'

'I wouldn't have thought sailing boats would interest you, Cassie,' remarked Ellie drily. 'You were always seasick whenever your father and I took you out on the water.'

'That was years ago—' began Cassie snappishly, but before she could say any more Romero explained.

'Cassandra was one of the hostesses at the show,' he said, smiling at her hostile expression. 'She was very good at it, too.'

'It was just a fill-in between parts,' protested Cassie resentfully. 'I don't usually do that sort of thing.'

'Don't you?' Her mother seemed to perceive that she suddenly had the upper hand. 'Remind me, Cassie: what was the last part you played?'

Eve now found herself in the unlikely position of feeling sorry for her and, with unexpected compassion she said, 'You had a role in the remake of *Pride and Prejudice*, didn't you, Cassie? I think you played one of the Bennett sisters.'

'You *know* I didn't play one of the Bennett sisters,' hissed Cassie, giving Eve a filthy look, but her mother only smiled.

'Mrs Bennett, perhaps?' she suggested, enjoying the

moment. 'You'd be unlikely to be cast as an *ingénue*, if that's the term they use these days.'

'So, did you and Mr Romero spend much time in Paris, Cassie?' Eve asked quickly, realising her grandmother wasn't about to back off, and this time Cassie seemed grateful for her intervention.

'Just a few days,' she said. 'But Jake promised to look me up the next time he was in London,' she added, giving him a forgiving look. 'And that was six months ago, wasn't it, darling?'

'Something like that.' Eve noticed that Romero didn't respond to Cassie's frequent endearments. But she was taken aback when he turned to her. 'And my name's Jake. Or Jacob, if you prefer.'

'Yes.' Aware that all eyes were on her now, Eve was forced to be polite. 'Yes, right.' Then, dragging her gaze away from his disturbing face, she managed to smile at her grandmother. 'Um—I'll go and see how Mrs Blackwood is getting on. Is there anything I can get you?'

'Yes, you can get me another drink,' said Cassie at once, holding out her glass as Eve got to her feet. 'I'll have whisky, if there is any.' She glanced at her mother. 'Your choice of wine isn't to my taste.'

'Nor are your manners to mine, Cassie,' retorted Ellie, and Eve wished now that she hadn't offered to go and see how the housekeeper was coping. There was an ominous atmosphere building in the room, and she dreaded what her grandmother might say next.

'I'm not a child, Mother.' Everyone must have noticed that the honeyed 'Mummy' had given way to the chillier term. 'And I don't like red wine, as it happens. But you knew that.'

'I'd forgotten,' declared her mother blandly. 'Your visits here are so infrequent, Cassie. I can't be expected to remember everything.'

Cassie's lips tightened, and Eve guessed she was biting her tongue. She must know better than anyone that it would be unwise to antagonise her mother when there was a guest in the house. Particularly when that guest was someone she wanted to impress.

In the hope of avoiding any further argument, Eve set Cassie's empty glass on the tray. Then, keeping her back to the room, she managed to sneak the whisky bottle off the tray and into the cupboard below. Swinging round on her heels, she said, somewhat breathlessly, 'I'm sorry. There doesn't appear to be any whisky here, Cassie. I expect there's a new bottle in the kitchen. Why don't you come and get it?'

The face Cassie turned to her was hardly friendly. Eve was sure the words, *Why don't you get it?* were hovering on her lips. But politeness—or common sense—won out, and with a muttered, 'Excuse me,' to Romero, she pushed herself to her feet and flounced across the room to join Eve at the door.

She waited until the door was firmly closed behind them and they'd put the width of the hall between them and the library before speaking again. But when she did, her words were hard and accusatory.

'What do you think you're playing at?' she demanded. 'I saw the bottle of whisky on the tray when Mrs Blackwood was pouring us all a glass of the poor excuse for claret my mother insists on serving. Don't think I didn't see you spirit it away into the cabinet. I'd be surprised if anybody missed it.'

Eve's lips twisted. 'I should have known that nothing I did would please you,' she said flatly. 'And here I was thinking I was saving your sorry ass!'

'What do you mean?'

'Are you for real?' Eve stared at her. 'Don't you realise your mother is just waiting for a chance to explode this myth you've created about yourself? You're a fool if you think she's forgotten—anything.'

'With your connivance, no doubt.'

Eve shrugged. 'If you want to think that, I can't stop you.'

'Well, what else am I supposed to think?' Cassie balled one fist and pressed it into the palm of her other hand. Then, less aggressively, she said, 'She wouldn't say anything.' A beat. 'Would she?'

'If you persist in baiting her, I don't know what she might say,' replied Eve honestly.

'But she's baiting me!' Cassie made a sound of frustration. 'Am I expected to take whatever she wants to give without defending myself at all?'

Eve moved towards the passage leading to the kitchen. 'I can't answer that. I suppose it rather depends on how much you want your—guest—to know about you.'

Cassie's mouth tightened. 'Are you threatening me?'

'No!' The look Eve cast over her shoulder was incredulous. 'Why should I threaten you? I don't care what you do, do I? How you conduct your life means nothing to me.'

Cassie scoffed. 'Little Miss Prim,' she said contemptuously. 'I wonder if my mother has any idea of the kind of life you were living before she arrived like a fairy godmother to whisk you away.'

'She knows,' said Eve, and without waiting to see if Cassie was going to follow her she pushed open the door into the reassuring light and warmth of the kitchen.

'Does she?' Cassie came after her, evidently deciding that if she couldn't torment her mother, she would torment

Eve instead. 'Well, don't talk to me as if you're Goody Two Shoes! We both know you'd do anything to get a man like Jake to support you.'

Eve gasped. She was used to Cassie speaking as if Mrs Blackwood was just a cipher, but this time she'd gone too far. 'You're wrong,' she snapped. 'I've never prostituted myself to get any man, Cassie. And unless you're prepared for me to expose all your dirty washing, I suggest you back off!'

CHAPTER THREE

IT WAS still dark—and cold—when Jake got out of bed. The heating hadn't kicked in yet, and he padded across to the windows to look out on a grey world, with only the silvery trace of a rime frost to soften the outline of the trees in the paddock.

He'd slept alone, much to Cassandra's annoyance. He knew one of the reasons she'd invited him here was because she wanted their relationship to advance to another stage. But he wasn't interested in that, and the fact that her mother had arranged for them to have separate bedrooms showed that she didn't approve of them conducting any illicit dealings under her roof.

She'd even phoned him on his mobile, evidently deciding it was too cold to brave the chilly corridors of the house when she couldn't be sure how he'd respond. Cassandra didn't like taking no for an answer.

A flicker of light in the yard below caught his attention. His room overlooked the back of the house, and as he watched he saw a figure detach itself from the building and head off towards the cluster of barns and outbuildings that were just visible in the gloom.

Eve.

Her tall, slim figure was unmistakable. Dressed in jeans and a bulky sweater, the thick braid of dark hair swinging over her shoulder, she moved with an unconscious grace that stirred an unwilling awareness inside him. Which was crazy. She wasn't beautiful in the way Cassandra was beautiful. Her features were too irregular, her mouth too wide, her nose too long. Yet she possessed an almost exotic allure that pointed to a Latin ancestry, and there was a wealth of knowledge in her smoky grey eyes. He'd found himself wanting to bring a smile to those full, sultry lips, to feel her warmth enveloping him instead of that argumentative old woman she worked for.

He hadn't succeeded. Not yet, at least. For some reason she'd taken an instant dislike to him, and try as he might he couldn't get her to relax. She'd been forced to be polite to him during the rather tense supper Cassandra and her mother had created, but he'd been conscious of her disapproval all through the meal.

He pulled a wry face. He would have to do better, he thought, without really understanding why he should want to. Nevertheless, he turned swiftly from the window and went into the adjoining bathroom. Leaving his shower until later, he had a quick wash, cleaned his teeth, and ran his damp hands over his hair. That would have to do for now, he decided, and with a grimace at his reflection he returned to the bedroom.

Pulling on his oldest pair of jeans, he shivered a little as the cold fabric encased his warm skin. Then, grabbing the cashmere sweater he'd worn the night before, he thrust his arms into the sleeves and jerked it over his head.

He left his room a couple of minutes later. He'd hooked his leather jacket over one shoulder, and his trainers made little sound as he strode along the upper landing. Downstairs, he hesitated in the chilly hallway, not absolutely sure which way to go. But then he remembered the direction Eve had been coming from the night before and, taking a chance, he headed along the corridor that he hoped might lead to the back of the house.

He was right. Or at least partly so. When he opened the door at the end of the corridor, he found himself in the kitchen. The housekeeper, who had just been about to take a tray of freshly baked rolls from the oven, looked round in surprise, and Jake guessed he was the last person she'd expected to see.

'Mr Romero!' she exclaimed, pausing uncertainly. But then, realising she had to complete her task, she hurriedly set the tray of rolls on the scrubbed pine table and closed the oven door. 'Can I help you?'

Jake gave her a rueful grin. He hadn't expected to encounter anyone else either. 'I—er—I was going to take a walk,' he said a little lamely. 'I wanted to get out back of the house.'

'Ah.' Mrs Blackwood pushed the rolls a little further onto the table. 'Well, you can come through here, Mr Romero.' She gestured towards another door. 'That leads to the bootroom. You'll see another door through there that leads outside.' She paused. 'But are you sure you want to go out so early? It's very cold.'

Jake could believe it. He was glad he'd brought his jacket with him. 'I'll be okay,' he assured her. He nodded at the rolls. 'New bread! I can't wait for breakfast.'

'You can take one with you, if you like,' offered Mrs Blackwood shyly, and, although Jake was impatient to get going, he couldn't refuse her.

'Great,' he said, selecting one with a golden crust. Then, after taking a bite, almost burning his mouth in the process, he grinned again and made for the door.

Outside, he discovered that she hadn't been joking. It wasn't just cold, it was freezing, and ramming the rapidly cooling roll between his teeth, he swiftly shouldered into his jacket. Then, after fastening the buttons, he removed the roll again and set off in the direction he'd seen Eve heading.

It didn't take long to reach the stable yard. Low buildings occupied two sides of a cobbled courtyard, with the black bulk of a barn dominating the other. And it was from the barn that he could see light emanating. It filtered out, a golden finger penetrating the half open door. If he'd been further way he wouldn't have seen it, the light swiftly swallowed by the lowering shadows.

He doubted she'd be pleased to see him, but he crossed the yard anyway, still munching on the crusty roll as he rounded the door.

Eve was in the process of forking clean straw onto a handcart. She'd pushed the sleeves of her chunky sweater up to her elbows, and as she bent towards the bales stored against the wall of the barn the back of her jeans exposed a delectable wedge of skin at her waist. But she didn't seem to feel the cold. Obviously what she was doing was keeping her warm, but he couldn't help wincing when she jabbed the fork particularly viciously into the stack.

'Ouch,' he said softly, and had the doubtful satisfaction of seeing her reaction. He'd startled her, there was no doubt about that, and a becoming wave of colour invaded her pale cheeks.

She straightened automatically. 'What are you doing here?' she demanded, and once again he could hear the barely suppressed impatience in her voice.

'I thought I'd take a look around,' he replied easily, finishing the roll and dusting the crumbs from his hands. 'What are you doing? I thought Cassandra said her mother had sold all the horses.'

'All but one,' said Eve shortly. And then, because she resented his impression that he could ask her anything he liked and she'd meekly answer him, she countered, 'Where's Cassie?'

Jake shrugged, propping his shoulder against the wall of the barn and putting most of his weight on one leg. 'In bed, I guess,' he responded, unbuttoning his jacket and warming his fingertips beneath his arms.

Eve's fingers tightened round the shaft of the fork. She couldn't help noticing that by opening his jacket he'd exposed the fact that his tight-fitting jeans were worn in all the most intimate places. The fabric clung lovingly to his shape, soft and textured, and she wondered why a man who apparently had an unlimited income would want to wear something so old.

She'd hardly been aware of how she was appraising him until her eyes returned to his face and encountered his. He'd been watching her, and in an effort to show that he hadn't fazed her she muttered, 'Don't you know?'

Jake's eyes narrowed. 'Don't I know what?' he queried innocently, and her momentary spurt of defiance faltered.

'Don't you know where—where Cassie is?' she said, lifting her shoulders in a dismissive gesture. 'I'd have thought you would.'

'What you mean is, you thought we'd be sleeping together, right?' he suggested mildly, evidently enjoying her confusion. 'Well, I hate to disappoint you, but I slept alone.' His eyes darkened. 'Very well, as it happens.' Which wasn't entirely true.

'Oh.' Eve swallowed. 'Well—good.' She turned back to her task and attacked the straw with renewed vigour. 'I have to get on.'

He straightened. 'Let me help you.'

Eve's lips parted and she stared at him with disbelieving eyes. 'I—don't think so.'

'Why not?'

'Because you—' She moistened her lips before continuing awkwardly, 'This is a dirty job.'

'So?'

'So—I'm sure you don't want to get all hot and sweaty.'

'I get hot and sweaty all the time,' he told her drily. And then, because he could see what she was thinking, he added, 'I meant working on boats, of course.'

'I know that.' Eve's face felt as if it would never be cool again.

'Okay.' His grin said he didn't believe her. 'I just didn't want you to get the wrong impression.'

Eve pursed her lips. 'I think that's exactly what you did want me to do,' she muttered, barely audibly. She sighed. 'Look, why don't you go for a walk and let me finish this?'

'Because I want to see this horse you're doing all this work for,' replied Jake, taking off his jacket and flinging it over a rusting oil drum. He came towards her and took the fork from her unresisting fingers. 'See, that wasn't so difficult, was it?'

Eve took a deep breath and stepped somewhat reluctantly aside. 'Cassie's not going to like it,' she warned, and Jake turned to give her a knowing look.

'Do you care?' he said, beginning to fork straw onto the cart with surprising energy. 'You know, I'm gonna enjoy this. I've been sitting on my butt for far too long.'

Eve thought about voicing another protest, but then what he'd said distracted her. 'I thought you were used to manual labour.'

'I am.' Jake loaded the fork and tossed its contents onto the growing pile on the cart. 'But for the past six weeks I've been trailing around Europe checking on orders, arranging contracts, and generally pushing a pen for most of the day.'

Eve hesitated. She badly wanted to know if Cassie had

been with him, though why that should be of any interest to her she couldn't say.

'Don't you have an assistant who could handle the grunt work for you?' she asked, and Jake straightened, flexing his back muscles as he gave her a narrow-eyed stare.

'Why don't you ask right out whether Cassandra accompanied me?' he said, massaging his spine with a grateful hand. 'That's what you mean, isn't it? Has Cassandra's mother given you the job of finding out what my intentions are?'

'No!' Eve was indignant. 'And whether or not Cassie went with you is nothing to do with me.'

'Okay.' His hand moved from the small of his back to rub the flat muscles of his stomach, and Eve's breath hitched when he accidentally pulled up the front of his sweater and a cloud of night-dark hair spilled into the gap. The pull of an attraction that was as unwelcome as it was primitive swept over her, and she had turned hurriedly away when he said, 'Well, for your information, then, Cassandra stayed in London.'

'Whatever.' Eve didn't look back. Squaring her shoulders, she said, 'In any case, that's enough straw. If you want to see Storm, it's this way.'

She slipped out of the door and Jake pulled on his jacket, feeling vaguely irritated that she was treating him so offhandedly. What had he said—or done, come to that—to warrant the cold shoulder she was presently giving him? No, scrub that, he amended shortly. She'd been giving him the cold shoulder ever since he'd got here, and he didn't like it.

Deciding that if she wanted the handcart, she could fetch it herself, he buttoned his jacket and followed her outside. The skies were lighter now, but it was just as cold, and he pushed his hands into his jacket pockets as he trudged across the cobbled yard in her wake.

The stables were amazingly warm. Considering only one animal was in residence, he'd expected it to be only marginally less frigid than the barn, but it wasn't. Unless the company had something to do with it, he thought caustically. Obviously Eve preferred the horse to him.

Storm was stabled at the end of the row. He'd evidently heard them coming and was neighing a welcome as they reached his stall. A solid-looking chestnut, the animal had a distinctive flash of white between his eyes. Intelligent eyes, too, Jake noticed, as it nuzzled Eve's pockets for sugar or some other treat.

Eve pulled out a small apple and let Storm take it from her hand. He crunched away happily, showing surprisingly good teeth for his age. In Jake's opinion he wasn't a young animal, but he looked strong and well-muscled.

'How old is he?' Jake asked, when Eve said nothing, and she gave him a scornful look.

'He's a she,' she said, unlatching the gate and attaching a halter. 'Storm Dancer. And she's twenty-eight. My— Mrs Robertson used to breed from her when she was younger.'

Jake stepped back to allow her to bring the horse out, and Storm took the opportunity to nip his ear. She didn't bite him. She was amazingly gentle, actually, and he saw Eve watching her with some surprise.

'She seems to like me, anyway,' he said, finding a reluctant humour in the situation. 'Sorry.'

'I imagine females usually do,' retorted Eve hotly, and then turned scarlet when she realised what she'd said.

'You don't,' remarked Jake drily, following her and Storm Dancer along the row of empty stalls, but Eve didn't look back.

'I neither like nor dislike you, Mr Romero,' she said, the words drifting back over her shoulder, but Jake could tell she wasn't half as indifferent as she was trying to sound.

'I'm pleased to hear it,' he said, as they emerged into the morning air again. He held her gaze when she darted a glance towards him. 'That gives me some hope.'

Eve swallowed. 'Hope—for what?'

'That you might come to like me.' He glanced about him, allowing her to return to her task. 'Where are we going now?'

'*I'm* going to take Storm into the paddock,' she told him, concentrating on controlling the mare to avoid another visual confrontation. 'I think you ought to go back to the house. Cassie will be wondering where you are.'

He glanced at his watch. 'At ten after seven in the morning?' He grimaced. 'I doubt it.'

Eve tugged on the halter, causing Storm Dancer to toss her head in protest. 'You'd know, of course.'

'Because I've slept with her?' suggested Jake flatly, and once again he saw that he'd disconcerted her.

But he also saw the way she tried to disguise it. 'Well, you have, haven't you?' she demanded fiercely, and instead of feeling angry he knew an almost irresistible urge to take her face between his cold palms and kiss her.

Her mouth looked soft and vulnerable, despite her desperate bid for control, and he wondered how she would taste. He already knew what she smelled like. She probably hadn't showered before coming to attend to the mare, and the clean scent of her woman's body was overlaid with the faintest trace of perspiration. He found it an incredible turn-on, incredibly sexy, but it wasn't a good feeling. Dammit, he'd come here with one woman and now he was lusting after another. What kind of an animal was he when he got a hard-on just being with Eve? What the hell was the matter with him?

The fact that he hadn't wanted to come here was some comfort, but Cassandra would spit blood if she even suspected he was attracted to her mother's companion. She'd been trying for more than six months to get him to commit to a relationship, and it was only because he'd had the excuse of business meetings in various parts of Europe that he'd been able to avoid any serious entanglement.

He liked her well enough. She was good company when she wasn't continually trying to get into his pants. And he'd been glad of her company at many of the parties and social gatherings he'd been invited to while he was in London. But this... This didn't bear thinking about, and, abandoning any idea of helping Eve to clean out the mare's stall and spread the fresh straw, he jammed his hands deep into the back pockets of his jeans.

'Does it matter?' he asked dispassionately. Then, deliberately emptying his face of any expression, he added, 'But I guess I'd better go and let her know I haven't forgotten about her.'

As if that was likely, thought Eve painfully as he strode out of the stable yard. She had the feeling that, however he felt about her, Cassie would make sure she was not easy to forget.

She wished she hadn't taunted him now. Although she knew she was asking for trouble, something about Jake Romero got under her skin. And, despite her determination not to let him get to her, she'd enjoyed their verbal baiting. Enjoyed being with him, she thought, tugging rather viciously at Storm's halter again.

And how sick was that?

CHAPTER FOUR

JAKE went up to his room, showered, and changed into navy chinos and a long-sleeved purple polo shirt. He was downstairs again, having breakfast in the morning room, when Cassandra finally made her appearance.

Of Eve there was no sign, but as it was already after nine o'clock he guessed she'd probably left for work. Mrs Robertson was still in her room, of course, resting her ankle. Which was a shame, he reflected, because he would have welcomed the chance to avoid a *tête-à-tête* with her daughter.

Cassandra trailed into the room, still wearing her dressing gown. A red silk kimono that she'd told him some admirer had brought her from Hong Kong, Jake doubted it was warm enough for Watersmeet in November. But he knew she liked the garment. She thought it flattered her fair colouring. And, as she didn't appear to be wearing anything under it, Jake guessed where this was going.

'Darling,' she exclaimed petulantly, 'where have you been? I came to your room earlier but you weren't there, and I was worried. Now, here you are, scarfing down bacon and eggs as if you didn't have a care in the world.'

'I don't.' Jake had got up at her entrance, but now he subsided into his seat again. He didn't usually eat a big breakfast, but Mrs Blackwood seemed to think he needed fattening up, and he hadn't the heart to refuse her. 'This is good.'

'It's also very bad for your arteries,' said Cassandra irritably. 'So—where were you?'

'When?'

Jake was being deliberately obtuse, but Cassandra was like a dog with a bone. 'Earlier on. When I came to your room,' she said, running the cord of her robe through her fingers. 'And don't tell me you were in the shower, because I looked.'

Jake finished the last morsel of sausage and put his knife and fork aside. 'I went out,' he said, relieved at having avoided another confrontation about their sleeping arrangements. Then, in the hope of diverting her, 'Why don't you get dressed and go and see how your mother is this morning?'

'Do I care?' Cassandra was bitter. 'She obviously doesn't give a damn about me. Did you hear her making fun of me—of my acting career last night? Just because I had more sense than to be satisfied with life in this provincial backwater, she takes every opportunity to make me feel small.'

Jake shrugged. He couldn't deny that Mrs Robertson had been provoking. But he didn't know the family history, so it was difficult for him to have an opinion. Eve was the one he felt sorry for—caught in the middle of two women who seemed determined to rub one another up the wrong way. Yet Eve had defended Cassandra to her employer, despite the way she'd spoken about her this morning.

'Anyway, it's early yet.' Clearly Cassandra had other matters on her mind. Coming round the table to where he was sitting, she loosened the kimono. It fell open, revealing that his initial suspicions had been right. 'Why don't we go back upstairs?'

Jake pushed back his chair and got to his feet. Then he grasped the two sides of the kimono in his hands. But, although he knew she expected him to pull her closer, he jerked the two sides together instead. 'Go take a cold shower, Cassandra,' he told her flatly. 'I want to go out and see something of the countryside around here. If you want to come with me, say so. I'll give you forty minutes to get dressed.'

He suspected she swore then, but he couldn't be sure of it. Whatever, she wrapped the kimono about her and marched towards the door. 'I'll need at least an hour,' she said, glancing back at him. 'Do you think you can entertain yourself for that long?'

It was not a good day. Fridays usually were, but today Eve found it almost impossible to concentrate on her work. The children knew it, and consequently played her up more than usual, and she was forced to use her strictest voice to bring order to the class.

The day didn't get any better when she was summoned to a staff meeting when lessons were over for the day. They never had staff meetings on Friday afternoons. Most of the teachers who were employed at the small primary school were eager to get home to their families at the end of the working week. But the head teacher's face was grave when she joined them in the staff room, and Eve had the uneasy premonition that whatever they were about to hear was not going to be good.

She was right. It appeared that Mrs Portman had heard, just that afternoon, that Falconbridge was to be merged with a larger school at East Ridsdale. The local education authority had decided that their school had simply not enough pupils to warrant the expense of keeping it open, and although every effort would be made to find the teachers new posts, by the end of next term Falconbridge Primary would be closed.

There was a stunned silence after Mrs Portman had finished speaking. The women who worked at Falconbridge—and they were exclusively female—considered themselves almost family, and the idea of being split up and sent to different schools was almost as bad for them as it was going to be for the children.

'But can they do this?' asked Jennie Salter worriedly. Jennie was a mother herself, and her children were still young enough to come to school with her. 'I thought I read somewhere that parents were fighting these closures.'

'Well, they are,' agreed Mrs Portman ruefully. 'But I doubt if the parents whose children attend this school will be prepared to fight our education authority—particularly if it means their council tax is going to go up. There simply aren't enough of them to make a difference.'

'So the school closes at Easter,' said Eve, her heart sinking at the thought of having to look for another job.

'Officially,' agreed Mrs Portman. 'But naturally I don't expect you all to wait until then to look for other posts. Besides, as soon as the news gets out parents will start looking for alternative schools. Not all of them will want their children to travel to East Ridsdale every day—not when there's a private school in the vicinity.'

'That's okay if you can afford it,' muttered Jennie gloomily, and Eve put a comforting hand on her shoulder.

'It's months away yet,' she said, trying to be optimistic. 'You never know—you may get a job at Ridsdale and then you could continue taking the children to school yourself.'

'Fat chance!'

Jennie refused to look on the bright side, and Eve couldn't really blame her. It was hard enough to find work in this area as it was, without a dozen other people doing the same.

In consequence, she was in a rather downhearted frame

of mind when she walked home later that afternoon, and she was in no mood to respond favourably when the Aston Martin swept through the gates ahead of her. Romero was at the wheel, of course, and Cassie was sitting proudly beside him, lifting a languid hand— almost as if she was royalty and Eve was just a paid retainer.

She wasn't jealous, Eve assured herself fiercely. She'd never had anything from Cassie in the past and she didn't want anything now. But just occasionally she wished the woman would acknowledge her responsibilities.

The squeal of brakes brought her out of her reverie. The Aston Martin had stopped and was now reversing back towards her. Oh, God, they were going to offer her a lift, she realised sickly. And she could guess whose idea that was.

A window was lowered and Romero looked out. 'Get in,' he said. 'We'll give you a ride up to the house.'

'That's not necessary,' said Eve stiffly, and Cassandra gave a protracted yawn.

'I told you she'd say no,' she declared in a bored tone. 'Come on, darling. Close the window, can't you? I'm getting cold.'

Jake's jaw compressed. Having spent most of the day humouring Cassandra, he wasn't in the mood to listen to her griping now. But, dammit, Eve wasn't making it easy for him either, and he was tempted to make some excuse and hightail it back to London before he did something he would surely regret.

Eve looked cold, he thought. Her exotic features were unnaturally pale in the light of the lamps that lit the driveway, and, although she was wearing a navy duffel, the coat didn't look substantial enough to keep her warm. He forced himself to suppress the irritation he felt at her evident unwillingness to allow him to help her, and, ignoring

Cassandra's protests, he thrust open his door and got out of the car.

'It's a good half-mile walk to the house,' he said, aware that Eve had taken an involuntary step backwards when he approached her.

Her dark brows arched. 'So?'

'So it's cold, and you look tired.'

'Gee, thanks.'

'You know what I mean.' His eyes darkened impatiently. 'I guess it's been a long day at the chalkface.'

Had it ever? Eve pressed her lips together, wondering why she was so reluctant to get into the car. It wasn't just because of Cassie, though she knew the other woman was watching her with coldly narrowed eyes. She just knew she wouldn't be doing herself any favours by allowing this man to get close to her.

'I need a walk,' she said at last, meeting his challenging gaze with more defiance than honesty. 'You go ahead.' She licked her dry lips. 'But—thanks, anyway.'

'I wish I thought you meant that,' he muttered, but short of picking her up and bundling her into the car, there was nothing he could do.

Then he remembered something, and, opening the car door again, he leant into the back and extracted the long black woollen scarf he'd bought at one of the mill shops they'd visited. He'd been glad of its warmth when he'd climbed the hill to the ruined Roman fort at Housesteads—Cassandra staying in the car, nursing the headache she'd complained about ever since they'd left the house—but he didn't need it now.

'Here,' he said, going back to where Eve was waiting and thrusting the scarf at her. 'Do yourself a favour and wear it.' And when she didn't say anything he added, 'We'll see you later, right?'

Eve nodded, but she waited until the Aston Martin's taillights were some distance away before unfolding the scarf and winding it about her neck. He was right. She did feel cold. But it was an inner cold as much as an outer one. Even so, the scarf was luxuriously thick and soft. Unfortunately, it also had his scent on it, an equally luxurious mix of expensive shaving lotion and clean male heat. But, despite her earlier misgivings, she buried her nose in its warmth and, after repositioning her backpack, thrust her gloved hands into her pockets and marched up the drive towards the lights of the house.

Thankfully her grandmother was alone in the library when Eve went to find her. Mrs Blackwood had volunteered the information that Mrs Robertson had insisted on phoning the hospital in Newcastle and cancelling the ambulance Eve had arranged.

'She said her ankle was feeling much better this morning,' went on the housekeeper ruefully. 'Then the next thing I know she's downstairs, pulling photograph albums out of the cupboard. When I asked her what she was doing, she said she was trying to remember what Miss Cassie looked like at your age.'

Eve stifled a groan. 'Did—did she say why?'

'No.' Mrs Blackwood shook her head. 'I expect she was just feeling sentimental, that's all. What with Miss Cassie being here and all. But she oughtn't to be doing so much at her age. I told her that.'

'No.'

Eve had acknowledged that fact, but now, when she let herself into the library and found her grandmother staring idly into space, apprehension stirred again. The old lady had something on her mind, and Eve hoped it was nothing to do with her.

'Hi,' she said, her own problems fading into insignificance when faced with a greater threat. 'I hear you refused to go and have your ankle X-rayed, after all. So how are you feeling now?'

Mrs Robertson blinked, and then stared at her granddaughter as if she was seeing her for the first time. 'I'm all right,' she said. And then, more gently, 'Have you just got home, my dear?'

'A few minutes ago,' agreed Eve, without mentioning the fact that she'd already been up to her room and put the scarf Jake Romero had loaned her into her wardrobe. She would have to give it back, but maybe not immediately. 'Um—Mrs Blackwood says you've been downstairs all day. If you insist on ignoring the doctor's advice, you should at least rest.'

'Because I didn't have that handsome young man to help me?' queried the old lady tartly. 'I managed.' She picked up the walking stick beside her chair and waved it meaningfully. 'I'm not helpless, you know.'

'All the same...'

'All the same, nothing.' Mrs Robertson sounded weary now. 'Stop grumbling at me, Eve.' She paused. 'Did I hear a car earlier?'

Which meant Cassie hadn't bothered to check on her mother, thought Eve unhappily. Didn't she care about her at all? Or, more importantly, didn't she realise she was playing with fire? For some reason, maybe because she was getting old, Mrs Robertson didn't seem to care what she said, and the previous evening's unpleasantness could be just the tip of the iceberg.

'Oh, I expect it was Mr Romero's car,' she said, striving for a bright smile. 'It—passed me on the drive.'

'So Cassie's back?'

'I imagine so.' Eve didn't want to get into a discussion

about her own encounter with them. She glanced about her. 'Have you had tea?'

'I didn't want any,' replied the old lady moodily, pushing the box at her feet out of the way and stretching her injured ankle. 'Where is she now?'

'Cassie?'

'Who else?'

Eve sighed. 'I expect she's gone upstairs to take off her coat,' she murmured awkwardly. 'She'll be down in a minute.' At least she hoped so. And without the disturbing company of her guest, if she had any sense.

'And has he gone upstairs, too?' asked Mrs Robertson evenly, although Eve knew she must know the answer to that as well as she did.

'Mr Romero?'

'Stop being obtuse, Eve. You know exactly who I'm talking about.' She paused, eyeing her granddaughter with shrewd grey eyes. 'What do you think of him?'

Eve swallowed, giving herself time to think. 'I—he seems—all right.'

'All right? What kind of an answer is that?' Her grandmother clicked her tongue. 'Don't you think he's too young for Cassie? She is forty-seven, you know.'

'Forty-six,' corrected Eve, before she could stop herself, and the old lady gave her a beetling look.

'Stop splitting hairs. Is she too old for him or what?'

Eve caught her breath. 'I—lots of women marry younger men.' She sought for an example. 'Look at Joan Collins!'

'Cassie is no Joan Collins,' retorted Mrs Robertson scathingly. 'And I don't believe I mentioned marriage. Why would he marry her when he can get what he wants without even buying her a ring?'

Eve felt her stomach tighten at the images her grandmother was unknowingly creating, and hurried into speech. 'So long as they're happy together,' she mumbled, wishing this conversation had never started. 'Um—would you like me to put these boxes away?'

'You know what's in them, of course?' The old lady arched an enquiring brow. 'I've shown you them before. Photographs. Some of them loose, some in albums. Your grandfather was very keen on photography. He said pictures are an incontrovertible record of the past. I thought I might show some of them to Mr Romero.'

'No!' Eve was horrified. 'You can't, Ellie. That would be malicious, and you know it!'

'Why?' Her grandmother was defiant. 'What's malicious about a few photographs? He might be interested to see pictures of what Cassie was like when she was a young girl.'

'You can't do that.' Bending, Eve gathered a couple of the boxes into her arms and carried them across the room to stow them in the bottom of the cupboard where they were usually kept. Then, straightening, she said, 'Anyway, I have something to tell you.'

'About Cassie? Or Mr Romero?'

'Neither,' said Eve tersely, hoping the sudden colour in her cheeks would be put down to her exertions. She gathered up another couple of boxes and stowed them as she spoke. 'According to Mrs Portman, the school is due to close next Easter.'

'No.' Her grandmother was shocked, and Eve hoped it would serve to distract her from thoughts of embarrassing her daughter. 'Why?'

'Oh, it's all part of the government's plans to make schools more efficient,' said Eve, stowing the last box with some relief. 'We've known for some time that Falconbridge is attracting fewer and fewer pupils, and those we have are to be transferred to East Ridsdale, which is bigger and more economically viable.'

'Since when has education needed to be "economically viable"?' The old lady made a frustrated sound. 'We're dealing with children here, not robots.'

'I know.' Eve came to stand beside her grandmother's chair. 'Looks like I'll be needing another job.'

'Just when you'd settled down,' exclaimed the old lady bitterly. Then, with a look of anxiety in her eyes, 'You won't move away, will you?'

Eve squeezed her grandmother's shoulder. 'As if,' she said softly. 'No, you're stuck with me now. This is my home.'

'You're a good girl.' Mrs Robertson reached up to cover her hand with her own. 'A better granddaughter to me than either Cassie or I deserve.'

'That's not true,' protested Eve, not wanting to get into Cassie's shortcomings again, but before the old lady could reply the phone rang.

There was an extension in the library and Eve went to answer it, not without some relief. Saved by the bell, she thought, picking up the receiver. 'Hello? Watersmeet Hall.'

'Could I speak to Miss Wilkes, please?'

'Miss Wilkes?' The woman's voice was unfamiliar, and for a moment Eve's mind felt blank. But then she remembered that Wilkes was the name Cassie used professionally. 'Oh, yes,' she said, making a quelling gesture to her grandmother. 'I'll get her for you.'

'Who is it?' the old lady asked as Eve made for the door, and she paused to whisper that it was some woman wanting to speak to Miss Wilkes. 'Cassie!' Her grandmother made no attempt to lower her voice. 'What does she want Cassie for?'

Eve shook her head helplessly, but she didn't have time to answer her now. Going out into the hall, she considered merely shouting Cassie's name up the stairs. But it was a big house, and it would be just like Cassie to pretend she hadn't heard her even if she had.

Instead, she ran up the stairs and hurried down the corridor to Cassie's room. A knock aroused no response, and with some trepidation she tried the door. Cassie could be in the bathroom and not have heard her, she reasoned defensively, but in any event the room and its adjoining bathroom were empty.

Sighing, she closed the door again, aware that there was only one place Cassie could be. In Jake Romero's room. And approaching that was an entirely different matter.

Even so, it had to be done, and, taking a deep breath, she walked back along the corridor to the room Mrs Blackwood had assigned to their other visitor. She knew it was on her grandmother's orders that the two rooms were some distance from one another, but, as both Cassie and her lover were young and agile enough to cover the distance without any problem, it was obviously a wasted effort.

Her first knock elicited a shrill protest, and her heart sank at the prospect of what she would find when the door was opened. But, to her surprise, it was jerked open almost immediately and Jake Romero confronted her—still fully clothed, she noticed a little breathlessly.

'Um—there's a call—for Miss Wilkes,' she stammered, feeling stupid—particularly when Cassie appeared behind him, draping a possessive hand over his shoulder. The older woman's sweater had been discarded, and her shirt was partly unbuttoned, revealing a tantalising amount of cleavage.

'A call? For me?' Cassie's brows drew together in some confusion. 'Are you sure?'

'You're the only Miss Wilkes here,' replied Eve shortly, recovering some composure. She started towards the stairs again, adding over her shoulder, 'You can take it in the hall, if you want some privacy. Your mother's in the library.'

'Privacy? In the hall?' Cassie snorted, forced to remove her arm from Jake's shoulder and button her shirt again with obviously irritated fingers. 'I mean, can you believe it?' she asked, turning to him for support. 'A house of this size and no phone upstairs. It's ludicrous!'

'I'm sure your mother doesn't find it a problem,' Jake retorted drily, aware that Eve's reaction to finding them together irritated him quite a bit, too. 'Go ahead. I need to take a shower anyway.'

'Oh, but we were—'

'You were about to go back to your own room,' said Jake flatly. He waited until she was outside, and then closed the door behind her with rather more force than was necessary.

CHAPTER FIVE

JAKE took the precaution of locking his door before going to take a shower. He didn't trust Cassandra not to come back after she'd taken her call, and the last thing he needed right now was for her to try and break the rules her mother had so subtly engineered. He didn't know why, exactly. It wasn't as if he couldn't say no. And since leaving London their relationship had definitely faltered, and he no longer had any desire to prolong it.

Perhaps it was seeing the way she treated her family, he mused, tipping his head to allow the hot water to rain down upon his shoulders. Cassandra certainly gave her mother little consideration, and if there was an argument that said the old woman deserved it, he was unaware of it.

As for Eve... Well, her situation was strangely ambiguous. She evidently worked for her living, and helped out around the estate when she could, yet there was an odd connection between her and the old lady that he couldn't quite put his finger on. There was affection there, and a gentle understanding. The kind of relationship, in fact, that he would have expected Cassandra to have with her mother.

But she didn't.

Had Eve caused the rift between them as he'd suspected on the journey here? She didn't appear to be devious in any way, but who was he to judge? He hardly knew the girl. But he did know, from experience, that appearances could be very different than they seemed.

Not least his own reaction to her, he admitted dourly, lifting his face to the spray. If she'd told him to his face, she couldn't have made her dislike of him any clearer. So why did he have this persistent need to show her he wasn't the bastard she apparently thought he was? Why, when she consistently provoked him, was he aware of her in a way that heated his blood and disrupted his sleep?

Crazy! Disgusted with himself, and with where his thoughts were leading, Jake swiftly soaped his chest and abdomen, suppressing a groan when he saw he was already half aroused. Dammit, what was wrong with him? Since when had he acquired this insane desire for a woman who had no interest in him?

He was drying himself when he thought he heard someone knocking at his bedroom door, but he ignored it. If it was Cassandra, he would be doing her no favours by opening the door. And if it wasn't...?

But he didn't go there. There was no chance that Eve would come to his door a second time. She'd made her opinion of what she'd found earlier clear enough, and, if he was honest, he would admit that that was what had initiated the soul-searching he'd indulged in during his shower. He resented it; resented her attitude. And he decided there and then that he'd had it with trying to humour her.

He dressed in narrow-legged woollen pants and a burgundy silk shirt. It was cold, but he'd found that Cassandra's mother tended to overheat the main apartments of the house. And, although it was chilly in the hall, and as he descended the staircase, he guessed the library would be almost uncomfortably hot.

He hesitated outside, not sure whether he ought to knock and announce his presence. But there was no light visible under the door, and he assumed he was the first to arrive. Without ceremony, he turned the handle and opened the door, and surprised a startled Eve sitting cross-legged beside the log fire burning in the huge hearth.

She sprang to her feet at once, reaching for the nearest lamp and flooding the room with light as he closed the door behind him. And Jake realised that any preconceived notions he'd had about her were just so much hot air. He couldn't ignore her; didn't want to ignore her. He'd been a fool to think he could.

She was wearing the same black cords she'd been wearing the evening before, but now they were teamed with a V-necked black sweater whose lace-trimmed neckline and bloused waist only hinted at the pert breasts he knew were beneath. Lamplight gave those smoky grey eyes an opacity he longed to penetrate, but perhaps penetration—of any kind—was not something he ought to be thinking about right now.

Nevertheless, just looking at her, at her pale exotic features and night-dark hair, he was arrested by the instinctive urge to know what it would be like to bury his hard swollen flesh in her softness...

Enough!

He almost growled the word aloud as she gazed at him across the back of the armchair she'd been using as a backrest, tugging a scarf of some kind from her neck. Evidently she'd been cold, even sitting in front of the fire, he thought, hoping he wouldn't regret not wearing a sweater. But then she held the woollen item out to him and he realised what it was.

His scarf!

'I tried to return this earlier,' she said, stepping forward to push it into his hands. She tossed the heavy braid of her hair over her shoulder. 'You didn't hear me.'

Once again he had to suppress the expletive that came

so readily to his tongue. If he'd known, he thought. If he'd only known it was Eve who had been knocking at his door...

But it was just as well he hadn't. 'I was probably in the shower,' he said, and saw the way her lips twisted at his words. She didn't believe him, he realised indignantly. She obviously thought he and Cassandra had resumed where they'd left off.

He wanted to tell her she was wrong, that it was because he hadn't wanted another argument with Cassandra that he hadn't opened his door. But he didn't. Instead, he moved towards her, dropping the scarf onto the desk as he did so, saying, 'How is Mrs Robertson this evening?' As if talking about someone else could cool his resentment. Dammit, she had no right to judge him. If he and Cassandra had chosen to make out on the front lawn of the house it would have been nothing to do with her, for God's sake. He glanced about him. 'I thought she'd be here.'

'No.' Eve didn't know what to do with her hands now that she didn't have the scarf to occupy them, and after an awkward moment she pushed them into her pockets. 'I expect she'll be down later.'

'Would she like me to—?'

'Carry her downstairs?' Eve interrupted him. 'No, I don't think that will be necessary.'

'Do you make all her decisions for her?'

His dark eyes were far too intent, and Eve moved a little uncomfortably under their regard. 'Of course not,' she said tersely. Then, moving purposefully forward, 'If you'll excuse me, I'll go and see if she—'

'And if I won't?'

Eve caught her breath. 'If you won't what?'

'If I won't excuse you,' he said softly. Then, his eyes

darkening, 'Come on, Eve, would it hurt you to keep me company for a few minutes? It's not as if I'm threatening to jump your bones.'

'You couldn't,' she asserted, hoping like hell that he wouldn't put her to the test, and his lips thinned.

'Don't be too sure,' he murmured drily, but Eve thought she could see reluctant amusement lurking at the corner of his mouth. 'You might do well to humour me.'

Eve shook her head. 'Why should you want me to?'

'Oh...' He considered for a moment. 'Perhaps I just want to know more about you. No harm in that, is there?'

Eve shivered in spite of the fire at her back. 'Cass— Cassandra will be down soon. She—she can tell you all you need to know.'

'I doubt that.' He gestured towards the chair behind her. 'Why don't you sit down and tell me yourself?'

'Perhaps I don't want to.'

'I'd gathered that.' His brows drew together. 'I wonder why?'

Eve expelled a nervous breath, but short of pushing him out of the way she was trapped. In more ways than one. With a sound she hoped he identified as frustration she stepped back and subsided into the chair he'd indicated with obvious ill grace. Then, when he made no attempt to seat himself opposite, but stood over her like some dark predator, she forced herself to look up at him. 'Well?'

Jake was intrigued in spite of her evident irritation. She was so aloof, so defensive, almost, and his earlier interest deepened into an attraction that had little to do with sex. Well, not a lot, he conceded honestly, aware that he was still sexually aroused by her cool, remote allure and, yes—why not?—her obvious reluctance to let him get close to her.

Why he should want to was not something he chose to

go into right now, and, realising he couldn't conduct a conversation from this angle—however advantageous it might be—he stepped across the hearth and took the chair opposite.

'So?' he said, when she made no attempt to speak to him. 'Tell me about yourself. Have you always lived in the north of England?'

Her shoulders seemed to sag at this question. But, 'No,' she responded shortly, leaving him with no choice but to ask another.

'Your parents lived in another part of the country?'

'I don't have any parents,' she replied. 'Is that all?'

'No, it's not all,' he exclaimed, annoyed in spite of his determination not to let her rile him. This was her way of avoiding any further conversation, and he wasn't going to let her get away with it. 'Everyone has parents, Eve. Or do you still believe babies are found under a gooseberry bush?'

Faint colour tinted the olive skin of her throat at this, and although he could defend his actions to himself, her sudden vulnerability wrenched his gut. 'I know where babies come from, Mr Romero,' she declared stiffly. 'Though maybe not as well as you do, I'll admit.'

Jake caught his breath. 'What the hell is that supposed to mean?'

Eve looked a little nervous now, and he suspected she'd spoken without considering the possible consequences. But she had no choice but to go on. 'I—don't have children, Mr Romero,' she said primly 'Perhaps you do.'

He was fairly sure that that wasn't what she'd meant when she'd made that earlier observation, but he didn't contradict her. 'No,' he told her, his eyes enjoying her confusion. 'I don't have any children. None that I know of, anyway.'

If anything, her colour deepened, but she wasn't about to back down. 'Not everyone cares one way or the other,' she said, surprisingly, though her gaze flickered away from his as she did so. 'In any case, for your information, I never knew my parents. My biological parents, that is.'

Jake frowned. 'You were adopted?'

Eve sighed. 'Of what possible interest is this to you?'

'Take my word: I'm interested.'

She was silent for a long moment, but then she lifted her head and looked him in the eyes. 'For a time,' she agreed. 'I ran away when I was twelve years old.'

Twelve? He couldn't conceive of it. At twelve she'd have been—what? A girl with pigtails in her hair? A rebellious pre-teen who didn't know when she was well off?

'I didn't get away with it, of course,' she went on. Her gaze was riveted on her hands, which were twisted together in her lap now, and he wondered if she was aware of what she was saying. 'I was found and sent back. Twice, actually. But I only ran away again, until the authorities decided it would be easier to let Social Services take the strain.'

Jake shook his head. 'But you were so young.'

'I was old enough.' Her lips pressed together, as if to silence any further confidences. Then, with a gesture of dismissal, she added, 'It all happened a long time ago. I'd forgotten about it.'

But she hadn't. He could tell. And he badly wanted to ask her how it was that she was living in the north-east of England now, with an old lady who didn't seem like anyone's idea of a social worker.

Then he remembered something Cassandra had told him. 'You're related to the Robertsons, aren't you?' he said impulsively, and was then taken aback when her face, which had been filled with becoming colour, paled to an almost luminous opalescence.

'Who told you that?' she demanded tensely, and Jake shrugged.

'Cassandra.' He was wary. 'Isn't it true?'

Any answer she might have made was prevented by the sudden opening of the door. Immediately the main light was switched on, further illuminating their erstwhile intimacy, and Cassandra stood in the doorway, regarding them with a look of unconcealed fury on her face.

She was wearing a filmy cocktail dress this evening, which clung to her shapely figure, and although it had obviously been made by an expert hand, it was totally unsuitable for a family supper at home. She had evidently decided to use any means at her disposal to get him to change his mind, thought Jake wryly, despising himself for his arrogance. And he wasn't entirely surprised to discover her seductive efforts left him totally unmoved.

'What's going on?' Cassandra demanded, staring at each of them in turn, and Eve felt as if they'd been caught out in some illicit assignation. Which was ridiculous. They'd only been talking, for heaven's sake. Though she was fairly sure she looked as guilty as hell.

Jake got to his feet without concern. 'Well, let me see,' he said drily. 'Eve returned the scarf I lent her this afternoon, and I asked her how Mrs Robertson was this evening. I offered to carry your mother downstairs again, but Eve thought that wouldn't be necessary. Then we spoke about—'

'I don't want to hear all your conversation,' snapped Cassandra shortly, and Jake arched enquiring brows.

'No?' he said blandly. 'But I thought that was what you did want. You asked what was going on.'

Cassandra glared at him. 'And you knew exactly what

I meant,' she retorted, making no attempt to mince her words. Then, as if realising they had an audience, she sucked in a frustrated breath before continuing, 'How long have you been keeping Eve company?'

Jake shrugged. 'Does it matter?'

Cassandra pursed her lips. 'You didn't think to let me know you were going downstairs?'

'I'm sorry.' There was an edge to Jake's voice now that even Eve could hear. 'I didn't realise I had to post my whereabouts. I gather you've been looking for me. That is why you're so—put out—isn't it?'

Cassandra's teeth ground together, but short of accusing him of conspiracy, there was little she could say in her own defence. 'I thought—I thought you might have wanted to know who rang,' she said at last, turning to close the door, exposing the fact that the gown had virtually no back to speak of. Then, turning again, she posed against the dark panels. 'You usually do.'

He could have argued with her. He could have said that the only occasion he'd wanted to know who rang was when she'd answered the phone in his hotel in London. But it wasn't worth the pleasure it would give her to put him on the defensive.

Nevertheless, he saw how her words had affected Eve. He wasn't surprised, therefore, when she got to her feet and said she would go and see if Mrs Blackwood needed any help.

When they were alone, Cassandra covered the space between them with flattering haste. 'Thank goodness she's gone,' she exclaimed, her tone much warmer now than it had been before. She rested her hand on the unbuttoned neckline of his shirt, her fingers touching his naked skin. 'You'll never guess what's happened.'

Jake lifted his hand and used the pretext of taking her

hand in his to remove it from his chest. 'So tell me,' he said lightly. He glanced across the room. 'But shall we have a drink first?'

Cassandra sighed. 'You don't understand. This is important.'

'Okay.' Jake released her hand and stepped back to hook a hip over the corner of the desk. He folded his arms. 'Go on.'

Cassandra moistened her lips. 'I've been offered a part in *Evermore*.' Her eyes were alight with excitement. 'Isn't that amazing?'

'And *Evermore* would be?'

'Oh, Jake! You must have heard of *Evermore*! It's one of the most successful soaps on television at the moment.'

Jake refrained from pointing out that, as an infrequent visitor to these shores, he seldom found time to watch the news on television, let alone a soap opera, however successful it might be.

But he couldn't steal her thunder, so instead he said, 'Way to go, girl! You must be excited.'

'I am.' Cassandra wrapped her arms about herself with evident satisfaction. 'So's Amy.' Jake knew Amy Lassiter was her agent. 'That was her on the phone, of course. I attended the auditions weeks ago, and I'd given up hope of hearing anything positive, but apparently the—er—the actress they initially chose has pulled out, so— '

'They chose you.'

'Yes.'

'And is it a big part?'

'Well, it's only for three episodes to begin with,' explained Cassandra equably. 'That's how they do these things. They introduce a new character, and if he or she goes down well with the viewing public, they expand the role.'

'Ah.' Jake nodded. 'So I imagine you'll be wanting to get back to London as soon as possible?'

Which would and wouldn't suit him. But it wasn't his call.

'Amy's asked me to go back tomorrow,' admitted Cassandra, biting her lip. 'There are so many things to arrange—contracts to sign, script conferences to attend, rehearsals and so on.' She shook her head. 'I can't believe it.'

'You're going to be very busy,' agreed Jake, aware that any feeling of relief he had at being let off the hook was tempered by the knowledge that he was unlikely to see Eve again. But then the door crashed open and Cassandra's mother, leaning heavily on her cane, came unceremoniously into the room.

'Sorry about that,' she said. 'Lost my balance as I reached for the handle.' She pulled a wry face at Jake. 'So—what was that you were saying about being busy?'

Jake had to smile at Cassandra's expression. She'd been put in the same position as she'd put Eve in earlier. 'Your daughter's landed a part in something called *Evermore*,' he told her smoothly. 'Here, let me help you to your chair.'

Mrs Robertson took his arm with evident relief, and their progress across the room was necessarily slow. But, after she'd subsided into the chair, she regarded her daughter with shrewd, if faded blue eyes, and said, '*Evermore*, eh? Well, well, who'd have thought it?'

'Not you, apparently,' declared Cassandra shortly. She seemed undecided what to do next, and finally settled on taking the chair opposite her mother. 'Aren't you going to congratulate me? This is exactly the sort of part I've been waiting for.'

Her mother moved her shoulders in a dismissive gesture. 'I suppose this means we'll be seeing even less of you in future.'

'Do you care?' Cassandra was bitter.

'Some of us might,' retorted her mother drily. 'But if it's what you want...'

'It is.'

'Then there's nothing more to be said. I wish you luck with it. Goodness knows, you've been out of work long enough.'

'I've been resting,' snapped Cassandra angrily. 'Honestly, Mother, I'm an actress, not a—a schoolteacher, for God's sake!'

Jake stifled a groan. He guessed it had been unwise of her to bring Eve's occupation into the argument, and he wasn't surprised when Mrs Robertson took exception to it. 'Eve has brains, Cassie,' she said scornfully. 'Which is something no one could ever accuse you of.'

'How dare you?'

'What? You think learning a few lines and repeating them parrot fashion in front of a camera requires intelligence?'

'I think you know nothing about it.'

'I think I wouldn't want to.'

'Can I get anyone a drink?' Jake knew he had to put a stop to this before they both said something they'd regret. 'Mrs Robertson? Some wine, perhaps? Cassandra?'

His words caused a pregnant silence that was almost as hostile in its way as what had gone before. But after a few moments Cassandra's mother seemed to remember her manners, and in clipped tones she said, 'Yes, a glass of wine would be very nice. Thank you, Mr Romero.'

'No problem.' Jake blew out a relieved breath. 'Cassandra?'

'Scotch. With ice, if there is any,' she said, barely

glancing in his direction, and Jake moved towards the tray of drinks with real enthusiasm.

He gave the women theirs, and then poured a stiff Scotch for himself. The single malt was smooth and sleek, and he welcomed the heat it brought to his stomach. It helped to banish the memory of the unpleasantness he'd just witnessed. He stifled another moan when Mrs Robertson spoke again. What now?

'I suppose you'll be leaving in the morning, Cassie?' she said, and despite the coolness of her voice Jake was sure she was trying to be polite.

Cassandra didn't immediately respond, and he hoped she wasn't about to rekindle the argument. But eventually she said, civilly enough, 'Yes. I have to be back in London tomorrow.'

'Ah.' The old lady absorbed this with unexpected interest. 'So you'll be fairly tied up for the next few days? What with rehearsals and such?'

Cassandra was regarding her mother warily now, and Jake didn't altogether blame her. 'I expect so, yes.'

'Hmm.' The old lady was thoughtful. 'Well, as you pointed out earlier, I know nothing about these matters, Cassie, but I'd have thought that in the circumstances you're going to have little time to entertain Mr Romero.'

Cassandra's jaw dropped, but she quickly recovered herself. Then, her gaze moving from her mother to Jake and back again, she said tensely, 'Why should that matter to you?'

'Oh…' Mrs Robertson shrugged. 'Well, it's just that I wouldn't like Mr Romero to feel he's not welcome to stay on here if he'd like to.'

Cassandra gasped. 'You can't be serious!'

'Why not? I understand he's quite interested in the area, and unless he has some pressing business of his own in

London there's no reason why he shouldn't stay and finish his holiday.'

'No!' Cassandra was on her feet now. 'I don't— Of course Jake is coming back to London with me.'

Her mother arched a provocative brow. 'Isn't it up to Mr Romero to make that decision for himself?'

'He can't. We—we drove up in his car.'

'He can always take you to Newcastle Airport. I believe there are frequent flights to London, and from your point of view it would be quicker.'

'You old witch!' Cassandra was trembling with fury. 'You think that by asking Jake to stay you'll ruin whatever happiness I have in accepting this part!'

'And your happiness is always the most important thing, isn't it?' demanded her mother coldly. 'It doesn't matter who you hurt, who suffers because of your—your selfishness, so long as you're *happy*! It doesn't even occur to you that Jacob might prefer to stay here. What are you afraid of, Cassie? That Eve might steal him from under your very nose?'

Jake didn't know what Cassandra might have done then if he hadn't stepped between them. She looked mad enough to scratch the old lady's eyes out, and, however much her mother might deserve it, he couldn't let that happen.

'Look, it's a moot point, anyway,' he said flatly. 'I can't stay on—much as I appreciate your invitation,' he added politely. 'Thanks, but I do have to get back to London myself.' He managed a rueful smile. 'Sorry.'

CHAPTER SIX

THE FOLLOWING MORNING, however, it soon became apparent that Jake wasn't fit to go anywhere.

Eve encountered him on the first-floor landing as she was about to go downstairs for breakfast, and one look at his grey face and streaming eyes was enough for her to advise him to go back to bed.

'I think you've got flu,' she said, not altogether easy in the position of surrogate doctor. 'How do you feel? You look—dreadful.'

'Gee, thanks.' Despite the humour in his tone, his voice was thick with congestion. 'But I'll be okay.' He paused before adding, 'Cassandra has to get back to town today.'

Eve knew that. Although it hadn't been mentioned during supper, her grandmother had confided Cassie's news to her when Eve had helped her up to bed.

'And do you think you're well enough to drive over three hundred miles?' she found herself asking, even though it was really nothing to do with her. Indeed, she would feel happier when he and Cassie had gone. But he was shivering violently, in spite of the several layers of sweaters he was wearing, and she went on doggedly, 'I could always drive Cassie to the airport. She can easily get a flight to London. It only takes a little over an hour.'

Jake pulled a wry face. Remembering Cassandra's reaction when her mother had made a similar suggestion the night before, he doubted she'd agree. But the truth was, he did feel bloody rotten. He could think of nothing more appealing at this moment than crawling back into his bed.

'Let's ask her, shall we?' he said, wondering how he could be sweating when he felt so cold. Perhaps it had something to do with the fact that Eve was looking at him without any animosity at last. But he wasn't going to go there. He was in enough trouble as it was.

'Let's not,' said Eve suddenly, apparently taking the initiative. 'You go back to bed and I'll speak to Cassie myself. I'm sure she'll understand.'

'Yeah, right.' Jake raked damp fingers through his hair. 'I wouldn't hold your breath.'

Eve pressed her lips together for a moment. Then she shook her head. 'Go back to bed, Mr Romero. I don't think you're in any state to argue.'

Leaving him to do as she'd asked, or not, Eve hurried down the stairs to the kitchen. 'Mr Romero won't be leaving this morning after all,' she told a surprised Mrs Blackwood. 'He appears to have flu. Do we have any hot water bottles? He can't seem to stop shivering.'

'I think you'll find a couple in the cupboard there,' directed the housekeeper, checking the bacon she had sizzling under the grill. 'So, will Miss Cassie be staying on, too?'

'I doubt it,' said Eve, filling the kettle and switching it on. 'I told you what Mrs Robertson said about Cassie landing this part in a television series, didn't I? I don't think she'll risk losing that.'

'But if Mr Romero's ill...'

'Well, we'll see,' said Eve, wondering if she was being too cynical. After all, from the way she behaved Cassie obviously cared about him. But roles like this were few and far between—even if it might mean leaving Jake to the care of virtual strangers.

And she still had to persuade Cassie that taking a plane back to London was the best option, Eve reminded herself. It was going to be no easy task, she knew. Of course Cassie might refuse to go, and confound them all. And from Eve's point of view that could be the safest option of all.

Leaving Mrs Blackwood to fill the hot water bottles and take them up to Jake's room, Eve ran upstairs again to find Cassie. She hadn't been in the dining room, and unless she'd made an early-morning call on Jake—which Eve didn't even want to think about—she was probably still in her room, packing.

When she knocked, however, she didn't get quite the response she'd expected. 'Come on in, darling,' drawled Cassie, evidently mistaking her for Jake. 'I knew you couldn't wait until we got back to town.'

It was too embarrassing to open the door after that, and Eve waited outside, hoping Cassie would realise her mistake. But when the door opened the woman was standing there in nothing but a silk kimono, and that was barely fastened across her naked form.

Her reaction was predictably explosive. 'What are you doing here?' Cassie demanded. 'If you've come to try and persuade me to apologise to that old bitch, forget it! She's seen the last of me this time. I won't be coming here again.'

'Unless you're broke,' said Eve drily. She had heard Cassie say much the same thing before. 'In any case, I haven't come to speak to you about your mother.' She paused, and then went on forcefully, 'Mr Romero's ill. He won't be able to drive you back to London today.'

Cassie's mouth dropped open. 'Jake?' she said disbelievingly. Then, with hardly more sympathy, 'What's wrong with him?'

'I think he has flu,' said Eve, noticing the way Cassie's

eyes narrowed at her words. 'He has— Hc looks—' She strove for a suitable word. 'Sick.'

'Are you sure this isn't some clever ploy of my mother's to keep him here?' Cassie was sceptical.

'Why should Ellie want to do that?' Eve was confused.

'Didn't she tell you she suggested he should stay on here for a few more days?'

'No.' Eve frowned. 'No, she didn't.'

'Well, she did.' Cassie was truculent. 'I wouldn't put it past her to have spiked his drink or something. Anything to put one over on me.'

Eve sighed. 'You can't spike someone's drink with flu,' she said impatiently.

'How do you know he's ill anyway?' exclaimed Cassie suddenly. 'Have you been knocking at his door again?'

'No, I haven't.' Eve was indignant. 'I met him on the landing as I was going down for breakfast. His eyes were all red and streaming, and he could hardly speak. Go and see him if you don't believe me.'

'Oh, I can't do that.' Cassic recoiled as she spoke, as if Eve was going to grab her and drag her forcibly along the corridor. She shook her head. 'I daren't risk it. I mean, I can't afford to get ill now, can I? What with getting this part and everything. If I were to get flu goodness knows what they'd do. They might even give the part to someone else.'

'I doubt that,' said Eve flatly. 'And people can't help getting ill. I'm sure they're insured against things like this.'

'Well, I wouldn't want to take the chance,' said Cassie firmly. 'I'm sorry, of course I am, but if Jake is ill then I think I'm going to have to find some other way to get back to London.'

Eve was appalled. 'Without seeing him?'

Cassie shrugged. 'He'll understand,' she said carelessly. 'I'll phone him on his mobile when I get back to town.' Then, with a lightning change of mood, 'You'll take me to the airport, won't you, darling? Mummy said there are regular flights to London from Newcastle.'

'Don't—don't call me darling,' said Eve harshly. But she couldn't argue with her. She'd already told Romero that she'd take Cassie to the airport if she was willing to go. 'You'd better ring and find out when you can get a flight.'

'Oh, God!' Cassie's expression changed again. 'A flight!' She gnawed on her lower lip. 'How much do you think that will be?'

Eve shook her head. 'About a hundred, I suppose,' she said tightly, not really wanting to continue this conversation. But she didn't have much choice.

'A hundred pounds!' Cassie gasped. 'My God, I don't have a hundred pounds, and my credit cards are maxed out.'

Eve half turned away. 'Not my problem,' she said, just wanting to get away from her, but Cassie wouldn't let her go.

'Couldn't you lend me the money, sweetie?' she asked wheedlingly, stepping out onto the landing. 'I'd pay you back. As soon as I get paid. You know I'm good for it.'

'Do I?' Eve was sardonic. 'How many times have I heard you tell Ellie the same?'

'Forget Ellie,' said Cassie irritably. 'This is between you and me, Eve. Come on. Don't you owe me?'

Eve could hardly speak. 'You—you dare to ask me that?' she choked, but Cassie just looked bored.

'Haven't you got over it yet?' she protested. 'You've got a cushy number here, haven't you? You wouldn't have had that if it wasn't for me.'

'I'm here in spite of you,' Eve told her bitterly. But even as she said the words she knew she was wasting her time. There was no point in expecting Cassie to understand. She'd never cared about anyone but herself, and she wasn't going to change now. 'All right,' she said at last. 'I'll lend you the money for the fare and I'll take you to Newcastle Airport. But only because I don't want you bumming off Ellie again.'

'You're a pal.'

Cassie would have closed the door then, but Eve put out a hand to stop her. 'You'll have to get an afternoon flight,' she said. 'I've promised to help Mr Trivett this morning, but I'll be free this afternoon.'

'Lunchtime, then,' said Cassie resignedly. 'Try not to be late.'

There was to be an autumn fair in the church hall the next week, and Eve had promised Harry that she would go to the rectory on Sunday evening and help him sort everything out. The fair was in aid of the St Mary's restoration fund, the church where Harry was minister, and in the ordinary way Eve would have enjoyed the visit.

She and Harry had become good friends in recent months—ever since he'd taken up the appointment, actually—and she knew he was hoping their friendship might deepen into something warmer.

Eve wasn't so sure. She wasn't convinced she wanted to have that kind of relationship with anybody. Ever. And it didn't help matters to know that this evening she would have preferred to stay at Watersmeet—just in case she was needed.

Not that she would be, she supposed, as she walked to the rectory after evening service. So far Jake Romero hadn't left his bed, and since delivering Cassie to the airport the day before her involvement in his recovery had been negligible. Mrs Blackwood had supplied him with tissues and aspirin and plenty of fluids, and according to her he'd slept most of the day.

'The man's exhausted,' she'd remarked the previous evening, setting a dish of steak and kidney pie on the table. 'And sleep's the best medicine of all, as my old mother used to say. You'll see—he'll be right as rain in a couple of days.'

Eve didn't doubt it. Romero was a powerful man. He wouldn't like being laid low by a simple virus. Besides, he'd told Ellie that he wanted to be back in London by the end of the week.

Her grandmother had spent most of the previous day in bed, too. Despite the feisty way she'd spoken to her daughter, having Cassie there had tired her, and Eve was glad she was being sensible for once. She had joined her granddaughter for supper that evening, but Eve suspected she was glad Eve was going out. It gave her an excuse to have another early night.

Harry Murray opened the door himself when she reached the rectory. A tall, angular man, with long, lean limbs and a receding hairline, he nevertheless had the kind of genteel good-looking features that invited confidences. Despite his age—he was only thirty-two—he was a popular figure around the village, and the congregation at his church had increased considerably since he took over.

'Hi,' he said warmly, stepping back to allow her into the hall of the building. 'You look rosy. Is it cold?'

Eve grinned. 'I'm not sure whether that's a compliment or not,' she said, shedding her duffel into his waiting arms. 'But, yes, it is cold. According to the forecast, it could snow later.'

Harry's expression grew anxious. 'I hope not,' he said,

hanging her coat on the Victorian hatstand and leading the way into his study. 'It would certainly limit the numbers coming to the fair. People are more inclined to stay at home in bad weather.'

'Well, the forecasters have been wrong before,' said Eve cheerfully, unwinding her scarf and looking round the large room with incredulous eyes. 'My Go— Goodness! You've certainly collected a lot of stuff.'

'Haven't I?' Harry looked pleased. 'That's why I'm so grateful to you for coming to help me.'

'I'm sure you know there are any number of volunteers waiting for an invitation to help you,' declared Eve drily. 'Not least all the ladies.' She pulled a face. 'You're considered the local heartthrob, you know.'

Harry flushed. 'You're embarrassing me,' he said, but she noticed he didn't deny it. 'Anyway, would you like me to get Mrs Watson to bring us some refreshments first?'

'Oh, no.' Eve shook her head. 'I've just had supper,'' she added, running a rueful hand over her stomach. 'Let's do some work first, and then we can think about refreshments.'

He agreed, and for the next hour they were absorbed in sorting out clothes and bric-a-brac and all the many magazines and books that the parishioners had donated. Eve enjoyed looking through the books. There was always something interesting to find, and she had to be firm with herself and not give in to the urge to browse.

Eventually Harry got to his feet and brushed his dusty fingers against his worn cords. 'I think that will do for tonight,' he said, looking round at all the boxes they'd dealt with. 'Yes, I'm sure I can manage the rest of it myself.'

Eve, who had been stowing tins of fruit and vegetables

into a cardboard box, looked up at him enquiringly. 'If you're sure.'

'I am.' Harry put out his hand and helped her to her feet. 'I don't want to spend the whole evening working.'

'Okay.' Eve extricated her hand and looked down at her own dusty fingers. 'But if you don't mind I'd like to wash off this dust first.'

'Of course.' Harry went to open the door for her. 'You know where the bathroom is. I'll ask Mrs Watson to bring us some—what? Tea or coffee?'

'You choose.'

'Tea it is, then,' he said apologetically. 'I'm afraid I'm not a coffee-lover.'

The word 'lover' sounded incongruous on his lips, despite its innocent application, and Eve was uneasily reminded of Jake Romero. That was what her grandmother had said he was: Cassie's lover. Eve shivered as she hurried along the hall to the downstairs bathroom. It was not a description she cared for—in any sense of the word.

She took her time, washing her hands thoroughly and brushing wisps of dark hair from her smooth temple. She needed time to compose herself, to put Jake Romero out of her mind. But it wasn't easy.

It annoyed her that this should be so, but she acknowledged that he had got under her skin on more than one occasion. The truth was, she'd never known anyone quite like him before, and she told herself she wouldn't have been human if she hadn't found him attractive.

Though only physically, she assured herself. Nevertheless, it wasn't pleasant to feel that he had some kind of hold on her thoughts. She didn't need the kind of complication he presented, and she wished he'd just gone back to London with Cassie—then she could have forgotten all about him.

Pressing her lips together, she regarded her tense reflection with impatient eyes. What was she doing, wasting her time worrying about Romero? After all, aside from the obvious barrier his relationship with Cassie created, what man was going to look at her dark skin and hair when he was used to Cassie's porcelain-skinned, blonde-haired beauty?

Folding the handtowel back onto its rail with taut, controlled movements, Eve turned to the door. Harry would be wondering what she was doing, and she could just imagine his reaction if she told him she was wondering what it would be like to have an affair with a man like Jake Romero. Dear God, he would think she was mad. And who could blame him? She thought she was a little mad herself.

Mrs Watson, his housekeeper, had already brought a tray of tea and biscuits, and when Eve returned to the study Harry was pacing agitatedly about the floor.

He stopped when he saw her, however, and his eyes took on an expression of concern. 'Are you all right?'

'Of course.' Eve did her best to control her colour. 'I told you I wanted to wash my hands.'

'You've been almost fifteen minutes,' exclaimed Harry, gesturing her towards one of the squashy armchairs that were set beside a low occasional table. 'Sit down. The tea's going to be cold.'

'I'm sorry.' Despite the fact that she'd expected such a reaction, Eve found herself irritated now. 'I didn't realise you were timing me.'

Harry clicked his tongue. 'I wasn't timing you,' he said unhappily. 'I was just—'

'Impatient for your tea. I know,' said Eve, managing a faint smile. 'Well, I'm here now. Do you want me to pour?'

'If you would.' Relieved, Harry took the chair beside her and stretched his long legs out towards the fire smouldering in the grate. 'You'll have to forgive me. I tend to be rather possessive where you're concerned.'

'Possessive?' Eve echoed the word rather uneasily. She didn't want Harry to feel possessive of her. They didn't have that kind of a relationship. Not yet, at any rate.

'Yes, possessive.' Harry put down the cup of tea she'd just handed him and leant towards her. 'Eve, don't you think it's about time we put our association on a more— formal footing?'

'Oh, Harry—'

'No. Hear me out.' Harry was determined to continue. 'You must know how I feel about you. I've made it plain enough. And—well—when I hear that you've got some strange man living in your house, I can't deny I get jealous.'

'Jealous?' Eve was appalled. She wouldn't have attributed such feelings to Harry. He'd always seemed so placid, so easygoing. And as for making his feelings plain... Well, the only physical contact they'd had was a fairly chaste kiss when they said goodbye.

'Do you blame me?' he demanded now. 'I've been expecting you to mention him all evening, but you haven't.'

'But—Mr Romero was Cassie's guest, not mine,' protested Eve, amazed that he should feel he had the right to question her like this.

'Yet Mrs Robertson's daughter has gone back to London, hasn't she?' Harry persisted, and Eve expelled an indignant breath.

'Yes,' she agreed tersely. 'Mr Romero has only stayed on because he's not well.' She endeavoured to calm herself. 'May I have a biscuit?'

'Of course—of course.'

Harry immediately reached for the plate, but in his haste he succeeded only in spilling its contents onto the floor. Red-faced, he bent to rescue the scattered biscuits, just as Eve did the same, and they banged heads.

'Oh, dear!' Harry was contrite. 'I'm such a clumsy oaf!' He caught her shoulders, forcing her to look at him. 'Did I hurt you?'

'Not much.' Eve tried to make light of it, but she was intensely conscious of the weight of Harry's hands upon her shoulders, and the quickness of his breathing as he stared into her eyes.

She knew she should have anticipated that he might try to kiss her, but she hadn't. She glimpsed his intentions only seconds before he bent towards her, and although she turned her head, he still managed to press his wet lips to the corner of her mouth.

'Oh, Eve,' he said, when she recoiled with a muffled squeak of protest, and, misinterpreting her reaction, he buried his hot face against her neck. 'You must know I wouldn't hurt you for the world.'

Eve couldn't get away quickly enough. His heavy hands and coarse breathing reminded her all too vividly of another man's sordid attempts to touch her. Scrambling backwards off her chair, she managed to put the width of the occasional table between them before saying unevenly, 'I have to go.'

'Eve!' Harry got to his feet, his face flushed now with a mixture of excitement and embarrassment. 'You can't leave yet.' He glanced down at the table. 'You haven't drunk your tea.'

'I don't want any more.' Eve realised she had to say something to normalise the situation, or run the risk of Harry suspecting there was something wrong with her. There was, of course, but that was nobody's business but her own. 'I've just remembered: I promised Mrs Robertson I'd be back by nine o'clock, and it's almost that now.'

Harry frowned. 'You didn't say anything about this before.'

'I forgot.' Eve managed to offer an apologetic smile. 'What a memory, eh?'

Harry still looked doubtful. 'This isn't because I kissed you, is it?' he asked.

'No—'

'Because if it is, I want you to know that my intentions are strictly honourable.'

'Oh, Harry!' Eve pressed her lips together with a genuine feeling of remorse. 'I—I didn't expect this, that's all.'

Harry shook his head in obvious bemusement. 'But I thought we were friends—'

'We *are* friends.'

'—that we understood one another—one another's feelings.' He paused. 'Don't you care about me at all?'

Eve sighed. She had hoped to avoid this conversation. Feeling her way, she said, 'I've just told you. I consider you a friend. A dear friend,' she appended, when her words failed to produce any lightening of his expression. 'But—well, it's too soon to—to consider anything else.'

'Too soon?' Harry sounded bitter. 'We've known one another for almost a year, Eve.'

'I know.' She was uncomfortable now, and she desperately wanted to end this awful post-mortem of something that should never have happened. 'I'm sorry, Harry, but I'm just not ready to—to think of you in that way.'

'It's this man, isn't it?' he exclaimed, with a sudden change of attitude. 'This—what was it you called him?— Romeo or something?'

'It's Mr Romero.'

'Romero?' Harry repeated the word scornfully. 'What kind of name is that?'

'He comes from an island in the Caribbean, and it's a Spanish name, actually,' said Eve, resenting his implication. 'And you couldn't be more wrong.'

'Oh, I'm not wrong.' Harry was unpleasant. 'A man like that is just the kind of man *you'd* be attracted to. Is he sexy, Eve? Does he make your pulses race? I should have known it wouldn't take much for someone with your background to be seduced.'

Eve's lips parted in dismay and she clapped a hand to her mouth to silence the cry of protest that sprang to her lips. That Harry, of all people, should say something like that, she thought sickly. My God, did he also know she had Hispanic blood?

CHAPTER SEVEN

HARRY realised his mistake at once—realised that he had said something completely unforgivable—and his face crumpled. His cry of anguish was still ringing in her ears as she wrenched open the door of the rectory and ran for home.

But Eve never faltered. Snatching her coat from the stand, she rushed out into the cold night air, not stopping to put it on until she was far enough from the scene of her humiliation for it not to matter. Then, shouldering her way into the duffel's reassuring folds, she wrapped the sides closely about her.

But she was still trembling, and she wondered if she'd ever feel warm again. That Harry, of all people, should show such prejudice made her feel sick, and she couldn't believe he actually thought she might be holding him off because of Jake Romero. What did he truly think she was?

The question didn't bear examination. Shaking her head, she reached the foot of her grandmother's drive more through good luck than management. In the first few minutes after leaving the rectory she'd hardly been aware of where she was going, and she realised it was a measure of the security the old lady offered her that had brought her unerringly back to Watersmeet.

She was chilled to the bone when she reached the house and, letting herself into the hall, she headed straight for the library. With a bit more luck Mrs Blackwood might have left a decent fire going in there, and she couldn't wait to toast her freezing toes in front of its warmth.

She'd expected the room to be in darkness apart from the firelight. As her grandmother hadn't got up for supper, and Jake Romero was still confined to his bed, she was surprised when she opened the door and found a lamp burning. To her dismay, she found their remaining house guest stretched out in her grandmother's armchair, a discarded magazine resting across his flat stomach. He had obviously been reading, but now he appeared to be gazing into the flames.

He had heard her come in, of course. The room was so quiet you could have heard a pin drop, and the magazine fell heedlessly to the floor as he got to his feet.

'Eve,' he said, his voice still a little hoarse, but not as congested as it had been a couple of days before. 'I'm sorry. I didn't hear a car.'

'I walked,' said Eve flatly, and although the idea of warming herself in front of the fire had lost its appeal, she felt too cold to leave the door open.

'You walked?' Jake was surprised. 'I thought Mrs Blackwood said that the Reverend Murray would be bringing you home.'

Eve didn't know what concern he thought it was of his, but she managed a swift shake of her head. 'I preferred to walk,' she said again. And then, because it was expected, 'How are you?'

Jake shrugged. 'I'll survive.'

Eve frowned. 'Does Ellie know you're up?'

'Ellie? Oh, you mean Mrs Robertson.' He shook his head. 'I doubt it.'

'Then—'

'I'm sorry, but I was going stir-crazy in that room,' he said ruefully. 'Mrs Blackwood told me you'd be out for the evening, so I flung on some clothes and came down here.'

Eve was sure he hadn't 'flung on' the chunky cream cashmere turtleneck, or the soft navy drawstring pants that clung to his hips and moulded the strong muscles of his thighs. As usual, he looked powerfully male, and sexy as hell—another first for her, she thought bitterly.

'Did you have a pleasant evening?'

His question had caught her unawares. He could tell that. Watching her, huddled back against the door as she was, he guessed he was the last person she'd wanted to see tonight. No change there then, he acknowledged drily, yet he had the distinct impression that she was pale beneath the hectic colour the cold had painted on her cheeks. And her eyes were wide and unnaturally bright. Almost as if she was on the verge of tears.

Dammit, what had happened? What had that old clergyman said to her? If he'd made a pass at her, if he'd touched her, he'd—

Yeah, right. Jake arrested his fertile imagination at that point. This was nothing to do with him. Even if the old man had raped her—which was taking his suspicions to unbelievable lengths—what could *he* do about it? She wasn't his responsibility, and he doubted she'd welcome any interference he might make in her affairs.

'Um—Mrs Blackwood said you were spending the evening sorting donations for some fair that's to be held at the church, is that right?' he persisted, when she didn't answer him, and Eve expelled a tremulous breath.

'The autumn fair,' she agreed in a low voice.

Jake nodded. 'Well, you look cold,' he said, when she didn't elaborate. 'Come and sit down. It's much warmer by the fire.'

'Oh, I—I might just go up to bed,' she said, declining his invitation. 'I am rather tired.' She turned towards the door. 'G—goodnight.'

Despite the urgent voice inside him that was warning him not to get involved, Jake couldn't let her go like this. Moving with more speed than he'd have believed himself capable of in his present condition, he strode across the room before she could get the door fully open, and slammed his palm against the dark panels.

The door thudded shut again, trapping her inside, and she turned to look at him with wide—fearful?—eyes. 'What—what do you think you're doing?' she got out, her voice betraying the panic she was feeling. 'If you touch me—'

'I'm not going to touch you!' he exclaimed, annoyed to find himself in the position of having to offer a defence. 'I'm concerned about you. Correct me if I'm wrong, but I think something's happened to upset you. Did someone lay his hands on you? Is that why you're jumping like a cat just because I stopped you from opening the door?'

Eve turned, but she did so without putting any space between her and the wooden panels behind her. She was obviously making every effort to keep as far away from him as possible, and, despite dismissing his worst fears earlier, he was now firmly convinced that—what was it Mrs Blackwood had called him? Reverend Murray?— Murray had assaulted her in some way.

'No—no one's upset me except you,' she said, but he could hear the tremor in her voice. 'I wanted to leave and you stopped me. What am I supposed to think?'

Jake blew out an aggravated breath. 'Well, you've nothing to fear from me,' he said shortly, straightening up and putting a significant distance between them. 'I merely wanted to help.'

'To help?' There was a note of hysteria in her voice now. 'You can't help me.' She swallowed. 'Nobody can.'

It was a strange response, but Jake didn't have the energy to pursue it right now. 'If you say so,' he said wearily, and she tilted her chin.

'May I go?'

'Well, I won't stop you again.'

'Good.'

There was defiance in her tone, and, wrapping her coat closer about herself, she turned towards the door.

But she didn't open it. Instead, despite taking hold of the handle, she remained motionless for several tense seconds, apparently staring at the wall. Then, to his amazement, she slumped against the door, sliding down until she was huddled at his feet.

Jake moved then. Although he still couldn't be sure she'd welcome his assistance, he had to do something. Dropping down onto his haunches, he put out his hand and tried to turn her to face him.

She resisted at first, flinching away as if he'd attempted to assault her, and his anger towards Murray escalated to even greater heights. He was sure now that the man was responsible for her distress, and he wanted to wring his scrawny neck.

Eventually he succeeded in drawing her away from the door, and when he saw the tears streaming down her face he couldn't stifle a savage oath. 'I'll kill that bastard,' he muttered, hauling her into his arms, and although there was still some resistance, ultimately she subsided against him with a shaky sigh of defeat.

She was trembling, he could feel it. And she felt so cold, despite the heavy overcoat she had clutched about her. Her wet face was pressed against his sweater, and as she breathed soft strands of silky dark hair brushed his chin.

Almost involuntarily, it seemed, he turned his mouth against her hair, tasting its lemony essence, inhaling its fragrance deep into his lungs. His hand was at the nape of her neck, and the temptation to tip her face up to his and taste her mouth, too, was almost overwhelming.

He scowled. Was he no better than Murray? he asked himself disgustedly. He wasn't thinking of her feelings any more. He was just thinking about himself. Just because the knowledge that she was cradled between his spread thighs was giving him a hard-on of painful proportions was no excuse for this depravity. He was only in the house because Cassandra had invited him, for God's sake, and he could just imagine her reaction if she could see him now.

He needed to get Eve to the fire, he reminded himself grimly. Not just because she was physically cold, but because she seemed chilled both inside and out. She needed heat, and brandy, not necessarily in that order. And he could do with a shot of Scotch himself.

In the ordinary way, lifting her slim, athletic form would have been easy for him. She was at least forty pounds lighter than the old lady, and infinitely less cumbersome. But his arms shook as he lifted her off the floor, and he cursed the fact that two days in bed had left him as weak as a baby.

Still, in spite of her opposition, he managed to carry her across the room and deposit her in the armchair he'd been occupying when she came in. Then, trusting her not to try and run out on him again, he walked across to the drinks cabinet on slightly uncertain legs.

Eve watched him from beneath lowered lids, scrubbing her cheeks with a tissue she'd found in her pocket. She didn't want to consider what a pathetic fool she'd made of herself, and, no matter how understanding Romero had been, she'd allowed him to get way too close to her. After what had happened with Harry she ought to have had more sense.

But she hadn't known how she was going to react when he'd guessed that Harry had upset her. His immediate anger with the other man, his instinctive belief that whatever had happened wasn't her fault, had broken down the guard she'd kept around her emotions all these years. She couldn't remember the last time she'd cried like that, and although she could make excuses for it, it still didn't alter the fact that Jake had exposed a vulnerability she'd tried so hard to erase.

He came back with two of her grandmother's crystal tumblers and held one out to her. 'It's only Scotch, I'm afraid,' he said, his hand not entirely steady. 'I couldn't find any brandy.'

Eve was compelled to take the glass from him, though she hated even the smell of whisky. She guessed lifting her had robbed him of what little strength he'd had left, and she couldn't turn him down.

'Thanks.'

He nodded, bringing his own glass to his lips and taking a steady gulp. 'God, I need this.'

Eve glanced up at him. 'I'm not sure that drinking whisky is wise in your present condition,' she said, dipping her finger into her glass and tasting the raw spirit. She grimaced, only just managing to hold back a moan of distaste. It was no better in small doses. 'You're supposed to be recuperating.'

Jake looked down at her with a laconic gaze. 'Yeah, well, this stuff will do me more good than all the hot cocoa in the world,' he replied drily. 'You, too. Drink it up.'

'Me?' Eve shuddered. 'I can't drink this. It tastes horrible!'

'Pretend it's medicine,' advised Jake, not taking no for an answer. 'It'll warm you up.'

'I am warm now.'

Eve proved it by pushing the duffel off her shoulders, and for a moment he was transfixed by the pure curve of her nape rising above the round neck of her tee shirt. The shirt was long-sleeved, and a dusty pink in colour, and blended well with the tight jeans whose waistband dipped below her navel. But he hardly noticed what she was wearing. Once again he'd been treated to a glimpse of her delectably smooth bare skin, and the arousal he'd felt earlier manifested itself again with record speed.

Thankfully she was too busy pulling her tee shirt down over her midriff to notice the sudden bulge in his pants, and, putting his empty glass aside, he took her glass from her and swallowed its contents in one gulp. Then, squatting down beside her to hide his embarrassment, he said, 'Are you going to tell me what happened?'

She seemed startled by his question. Perhaps she'd hoped the Scotch would divert him—or her amateur attempt to focus his attention on his health. Either way, it hadn't worked. If he managed to put thoughts of her naked out of his mind, he was instantly reminded of her dipping a finger into her glass. God, did she have any idea how provocative that action was? Somehow he doubted it, yet there was an odd look of wary perception in her eyes.

'What happened when?' she countered now, and Jake guessed she was still hoping to avoid a confrontation. She grimaced. 'I must have got really chilled. I don't usually fall apart like that.'

'Eve!' Ignoring her immediate withdrawal, he put out his hand and captured her chin between his thumb and forefinger. 'Your falling apart, as you put it, had nothing to do with the cold and everything to do with the Reverend Murray. Just tell me what the old fool did, for God's sake. Did he hurt you?'

Eve tried to jerk her chin away from his hand, and when that didn't work she adopted a disdainful stare. 'Harry isn't old,' was all she said, in a scornful voice. 'He's probably younger than you are.'

Jake let her go then, surging to his feet in angry disbelief. What the hell was she saying? That while he'd been picturing her at the mercy of some perverted old lecher, she'd actually spent the evening with a man who might conceivably have expected a different response to his advances?

'So what really happed?' he demanded, looking down at her coldly, unable to hide the resentment in his gaze. 'A lovers' fight? A disagreement? Or has he dumped you for someone else?'

Eve winced as if he'd struck her, and all the earlier empathy he'd felt on her behalf came flooding back with renewed strength. Dammit, he hadn't been mistaken. Something had happened, something bad, and he'd only made it worse with his crass accusations.

'Eve—' he began, but she was already getting to her feet, gathering her coat against her, looking anywhere but at him. God, he thought, how could he have been so stupid? It would have taken more than a quarrel with her boyfriend to destroy the cool self-possession she always exhibited towards him.

'Eve, I'm sorry,' he started again, but she wasn't listening, moving past him with her eye on the door and the evident intention of putting as much space between them as possible.

He expelled a harsh breath. He couldn't let her go like this. He had to make her see that he'd felt betrayed when she'd told him that Murray was a young man, that his amateurish attempt at chivalry had been blunted by the realisation that she was—might be—involved with some-one.

The ramifications of that statement were too compli-cated to consider now. Nor did he choose to remember that Eve's affairs—her well-being—had nothing to do with him. Or what he was admitting by feeling as he did. He just knew that if he allowed her to walk out of this room without accepting his apology he'd never forgive himself.

Gritting his teeth against the anticipation of failure, he reached out and snagged a corner of her coat sleeve as she brushed past him. 'Wait!'

She yanked at the sleeve, and when she couldn't get him to release it, she simply dropped the coat on the floor and stumbled over it. Swearing, he stepped over the coat and managed to catch her wrist instead. 'Eve, please,' he said imploringly, forcing her to a standstill. 'You've got to give me a chance to explain.'

'What's to explain?' He could only marvel at the strength of will that forced her to lift her head and meet his gaze. 'I assume you think it's all right for a man to maul a woman he's supposed to have some respect for?'

'No!' Jake was appalled. 'Is that what he did?' He sought for a suitable way to describe it that didn't involve mentioning sex while he entertained methods of revenge all over again. 'I guess he—took advantage of you, right?'

Eve looked as if she didn't want to answer him. But then she blurted out painfully, 'He kissed me!'

She knew what he would think as soon as she said it. After all, what was a simple kiss between friends? How could she explain the outrage she'd felt when Harry had grabbed her and pressed his wet lips against hers without sounding paranoid? Jake knew nothing of her history. And she certainly had no intention of telling him now.

'He kissed you?' he echoed, and although he was trying to keep the incredulity out of his voice she knew it was there, just beneath the surface.

'Yes, he kissed me,' she said, trying to stare him out and not succeeding. 'I suppose you think that makes me some kind of a screwball, getting het-up over something so—so unimportant.'

Jake's eyes narrowed. 'But it wasn't unimportant to you,' he said, with more shrewdness than she'd given him credit for. 'Was it?'

Eve put up a nervous hand and tugged on a strand of hair that had escaped from her braid. 'It wasn't the kiss,' she admitted at last. 'It was what came after.' She didn't want to go on, but he had been kind and he deserved some kind of an explanation. 'He— Because I objected, he accused me of preferring someone else.'

Jake stared at her warily. Dammit, he'd been imagining she had few friends, holed up here with an argumentative old woman, but now it appeared that not only did she have an admirer, she apparently had more than one. It shouldn't, but it irritated the hell out of him.

'I see,' he said at last, and, realising he still had her wrist in a death grip, relaxed his hold. 'And do you? Prefer someone else?'

Eve's face flamed. 'No.'

'So you just—what? Don't like men in general?'

'No!' Eve snatched her wrist out of his grasp and rubbed it vigorously, as if to remove any trace of his scent from her skin. 'I just don't like being—touched.'

'I can see that.' Jake's voice was harsh to his ears, and he wondered if it was the unaccustomed amount of Scotch he'd consumed in a short time that was constricting his vocal cords. 'So, is this how you reacted when Murray touched you? Because I have to say it's damn demeaning to have someone behave as if you had some lethal infection.'

'I didn't.' Despite her efforts to maintain a semblance of composure, the accusation caught her on the raw. 'You don't understand.'

'So make me.'

'I can't.'

'Or won't.'

She shook her head. 'Why should you care about me?'

'Damned if I know, but I do.'

The atmosphere was suddenly electric. Jake didn't know if he was imagining it, or whether some chemical reaction had been activated by his words. Whatever—and with a lack of restraint he deplored later—he moved until there was barely an inch of space between them. Then, looking down into her startled face, he said thickly, 'Touch me. I promise I won't bite.'

Eve shook her head, but she didn't move away. 'This is crazy.'

'Agreed.' His eyes travelled lower, to the tantalising glimpse of olive skin exposed again above her navel. 'But just do it, eh?' He grimaced. 'To save my feelings if nothing else.'

Eve's breath came out in a rush. 'I don't believe anything I've done has hurt your feelings,' she said, the tip of her tongue appearing to moisten her lower lip. 'But if it has, I'm sorry.'

'Prove it.'

'How?'

How indeed? Jake hoped he wasn't being too ambitions in thinking he could cure something that had obviously been some years in the making. He had no real experience of phobias or psychological problems. He just sensed that whatever major hang-ups she had, they weren't going to go away by simply ignoring them.

'Come closer,' he said, hoping he wasn't being too optimistic in thinking he could control the situation.

Just standing close to her like this, inhaling the womanly scents of her body, was amazingly erotic. Images of the hot, steamy sex they could have shared if the circumstances had been different were enough to make him dizzy. And it was becoming increasingly hard to remember exactly who she was and why he was here.

'I think I should leave now,' she said abruptly, and Jake wondered if she'd read his mind. 'Thank you for—for listening to me. And you're right. I probably overreacted. In his defence, I have to say that Harry's never done anything to upset me before.'

To hell with Harry! Jake only just stopped himself from saying it out loud. He'd be happy if he never heard the man's name again.

'I don't recall saying you'd overreacted,' he said instead, his hands balling into fists at his sides. 'And I don't know what the bastard said, because you won't tell me me.'

'It wasn't important,' she insisted, taking a significant step back from him. Jake's hands rose almost automatically to prevent her from moving away.

'It was important enough to make you cry,' he reminded her savagely, and before he could prevent it his hands had settled on the bared skin at her waist.

He didn't know who was the most shocked—herself or him. He hadn't intended to touch her; dammit, she'd just spent the last fifteen minutes explaining that she didn't like to be touched. But as soon as his fingers met skin that was soft and warm and unbelievably smooth, any doubts he'd had about the sanity of what he was about to do went out of the window.

'Don't,' she said, the word torn from her lips, and he thought how pointless the protest was. In her agitation to avoid him her chest was heaving, and the hard peaks of her breasts were clearly visible beneath her tee shirt. She was irresistible, he thought. Irresistible and available. And, abandoning any attempt at playing the hero, he bent his head and covered her lips with his.

She tasted like heaven. That was his first thought. Her mouth was hot and deliciously vulnerable. Her breathing was uneven, short gasps that he inhaled deep into his lungs. She didn't touch him, even though he must have caught her off balance, but he couldn't ignore the fact that her breasts were crushed against his chest and her thighs were moving restlessly against his.

It wasn't the reaction he'd anticipated. He had to admit he'd expected her to fight him all the way. But, apart from feeling a little stiff, she acquiesced to his hungry kiss without obvious resistance. And he came to what he later realised was an arrogant conclusion that it wasn't being touched that bugged her, it was being touched by the wrong man.

The idea was exhilarating—the possibilities endless. Growing bolder, he slipped his tongue between her teeth and deepened the kiss. But his head swam with sudden dizziness as he explored her mouth, and he realised at once how weak he still was. He was swaying on his feet now, and he thanked God she hadn't tried to fight him off. If she had, he wouldn't have stood a chance.

His humiliation came swiftly and devastatingly. When he thought about it later he knew he should have guessed that nothing was ever that easy. Eve hadn't been acquiescent; she'd just been biding her time. The moment he showed his vulnerability, she was ready to strike.

He was shaking, his legs trembling with the effort of supporting his weight. He lifted his head, blinking in an effort to focus his swimming senses, and Eve immediately tried to take her revenge.

And she would have succeeded, too, if he hadn't chosen that moment to drag himself away from her. Bending forward, he was struggling to get his breath at the same moment that she brought her knee up between his legs. As it was, the crippling blow merely brushed its objective, but it was enough to send him staggering back against the desk.

He groaned, he remembered later, more because of his heaving lungs than her success. Nevertheless, she seemed to think she'd achieved what she'd wanted, and, snatching up her coat, she wrenched open the door and ran out of the room.

CHAPTER EIGHT

LIGHT filtering through a crack in the curtains got Eve out of bed. Dear God, she wondered, what time was it? It was usually still dark when she woke up.

Fumbling for her watch, she stumbled across to the windows and drew the curtain aside. Brilliant sunlight spilled into the room and a glance at her watch showed her that it was almost ten o'clock.

Ten o'clock! She was horrified. She'd overslept. Or rather, she hadn't. Remembering that she hadn't fallen asleep until well into the early hours, it was no wonder that she'd slept in.

Still, that didn't alter the fact that this was a working day—and, bearing in mind that Falconbridge Primary was due to close, she was hardly doing herself any favours by missing lessons. What kind of a report was that to put in her reference?

Downstairs, after a swift shower, Eve told the startled housekeeper that she wouldn't have time for breakfast. 'Oh, but Mr Romero said to let you sleep on,' Mrs Blackwood protested, and Eve felt an uneasy pang. What else had 'Mr Romero' told her? she wondered. And, in God's name, how was she supposed to face him after what had happened the night before?

'Where—where is Mr Romero?' she asked faintly, hoping she wouldn't have to see him before she left for school. Maybe almost twenty-four hours would be enough to blunt the memory of what she'd done.

What *she'd* done?

'Er—don't you know?' Mrs Blackwood was speaking again, and Eve tried to concentrate. 'I thought you must have said your goodbyes last evening. He left—' she glanced at the kitchen clock '—it must have been about half-past eight.'

'He left?' Eve was confused. 'What—you mean he's gone out?'

'He's gone back to London,' Mrs Blackwood informed her regretfully. 'I said I didn't think he was well enough to drive all that way, but he insisted he had to go. He must have had a call or something. On his mobile phone, you know. Maybe it was from Miss Cassie. Whatever—it was none of my business.'

'No.' Eve felt a sudden wave of depression sweep over her. 'Well, I'd better go and tell Ellie he's gone.'

'Oh, she knows,' said Mrs Blackwood airily. 'Mr Romero had a word with her before he left.' She pulled a face. 'Madam didn't approve, any more than I did, but what could she do? He was determined to go.'

Eve's shoulders sagged. 'I see.'

'Are you all right?' The housekeeper was looking at her anxiously now. 'You're very pale. Are you sure you're not coming down with the same complaint Mr Romero had?'

'You mean flu?' Eve could hear the irony in her voice. 'No, I'm all right. Just tired, that's all.'

'Well, you look after yourself,' advised Mrs Blackwood severely. 'And going without breakfast is a silly thing to do in the circumstances.'

'I'll get a coffee at school,' Eve assured her, hoping she wouldn't be too late for morning break. 'See you later.'

Despite the sunshine, it was still cold, and Eve walked briskly down the drive. She could have used her grand-

mother's Wolseley, but the old car was so cumbersome
to handle that she usually preferred to walk. Besides, her
mind was busy with other things, and she wouldn't have
trusted herself behind the wheel of such a lethal weapon.

Depressingly, it didn't help to know that by leaving
Romero had removed any embarrassment she might have
felt at seeing him again. Despite what she'd thought earlier, deep inside she'd wanted to speak to him, to assure
herself that she hadn't caused him any permanent damage
by her reckless actions. Silly, perhaps, after the way he'd
behaved, but she feared her punishment had been out of
all proportion to his offence.

She caught her breath suddenly. Yet how could she feel
that way? Compared to Jake Romero's, Harry's behaviour
seemed almost innocent—his desire to prove his love for
her the complete opposite of the other man's intentions.

So why did she care if she'd hurt him? If she'd really
been revolted when Jake touched her, it shouldn't matter
that she was never going to see him again.

But, unfortunately, it wasn't that simple. In her heart
of hearts she knew that for the first time in her life she'd
felt feelings stir inside her that she'd hardly known ex-
isted. And the truth was, if he hadn't shown how weak
he was, how easy it would be for her to hurt him, she
actually might have given in.

But to what? After all these years of keeping men at
arm's length, did she really know? Oh, she knew about
sex, about what a man wanted and how far he was prepared to go to get it, but even she could see that what had
happened the night before had been nothing like that.

She really knew nothing about consensual sex, about
consensual relationships—the kind Cassie had with her
many conquests, for example. The kind she'd had—was
still having—with Jake Romero.

Eve shivered. If nothing else, that should convince her that she'd made the right decision. Whatever Romero had wanted, it was not something she could supply, and she ought to be glad that he'd left before she did something she'd regret.

All the same, that didn't stop her from thinking about him during the endless day that followed.

Mrs Portman was unexpectedly understanding when Eve explained, truthfully, that she'd slept badly and that that was why she was late. But Eve could have wished that she'd ranted and raved and given her something else to worry about instead of what might have been.

The memory of how she'd felt when Jake kissed her followed her into her sleep for that night and many nights to come. And no matter how rational she could be in daylight hours, her subconscious persisted in relieving the sensuous brush of his aroused body against hers and the consuming hunger of his mouth.

Jake went home for Christmas. Alone.

Since his return to London at the end of November he'd succeeded in avoiding any intimate meetings with Cassandra. And, although she expressed her irritation in frequent phone calls, usually late at night after she'd finished at the television studios, thankfully the producers of the tri-weekly soap were pleased with her, and that had mollified her complaints.

For his part, Jake had no sensible explanation for his sudden aversion to her company. Oh, sure, he hadn't liked the way she treated her mother, but he'd never before considered familial loyalties a prerequisite in a girlfriend. His abortive first marriage had taught him that families could be both a blessing and a curse, and since then he'd avoided all attempts to introduce that kind of complication to a relationship.

So why had he agreed to go to Northumberland with Cassandra? A less cynical observer than himself might contend that the visit had been preordained, that it was the only way he could have met Eve, but he wasn't prepared to accept that theory. For God's sake, the girl had hated him on sight, and after the way she'd reacted to his lovemaking there was no earthly reason why he should want to see her again.

But he did.

Which was one of the reasons why he went back to San Felipe for Christmas. Not the main reason, he assured himself. That had to do with still feeling hungover from his dose of flu and needing some well-deserved sunshine after too many weeks spent in Europe in winter.

Even so, he hadn't intended to go. The British Boat Show was held at the beginning of January, and it would have been far more sensible to wait until it was over before returning home. As it was, he condemned himself to two long-haul flights in less than two weeks, and aroused Cassandra's fury for not thinking about her at all.

Not that her feelings had been high on his agenda of things to consider when he'd been planning his trip. On the contrary, his thoughts had been filled with images of another young woman, spending the holiday season in a cold and inhospitable climate with only two elderly women for company.

And Harry Murray, he reminded himself savagely. After the way he'd behaved, she'd probably revised her opinion of the sainted vicar of St Mary's.

He arrived back from his short holiday to find a handful of messages from Cassandra waiting for him at his hotel. Evidently she'd been calling him for the past three days.

He stuffed the slips the receptionist gave him into his pocket, deciding he'd read them when he wasn't depressed and jet-lagged. Right now, all he wanted was a shower, a stiff drink and his bed, in that order, and anything Cassandra had to say could surely wait until the following morning.

Despite the fact that it was only the middle of the morning, Jake took a shower, drew his curtains, poured himself a half-tumbler of Scotch from the bottle the Room Service waiter had left on the table, and tumbled into bed.

He fell asleep immediately for once, and he wasn't best pleased when less than an hour later the phone beside his bed shrilled its strident tone.

'Dammit!' he muttered, trying to reach the receiver without lifting his head from the pillow. But all he succeeded in doing was knocking it to the floor, and, swearing again, he hauled himself up and down. 'Yeah?' he said, when he got the handset to his ear. 'This had better be good.'

'Jake? Darling? Is that you?'

Cassandra! Jake scowled and flung himself back on his pillows. He might have known. He should have told the receptionist to hold all calls until the following day. As it was, short of lying to her, he could hardly deny he was there.

'Cassandra,' he said, hoping she would hear the censure in his voice. 'I was going to ring you later.' Liar! 'When I got up.'

'Oh.' She seemed nonplussed for a moment. 'You're in bed? But it's eleven-thirty in the morning.'

'It's only five-thirty in San Felipe,' he said, holding onto his temper with an effort. 'I just got back.'

'Oh, yes. I know. The receptionist at the hotel told me you were expected back today.'

'Really?' Jake would have a word with the receptionist concerned when he had the chance.

'Yes, really.' Cassandra didn't seem to notice the edge in his tone. 'I suppose she felt sorry for me. I've been trying to reach you for days. I thought you said you'd be back on the second?'

'It's only the fifth,' said Jake tersely. 'I got a later flight.'

'Yes.' Cassandra hesitated a moment. 'So—you're in bed at this minute?'

'I think I just said so.'

'Well, would you like me to come round, then? I could give you a massage. Did I tell you? One of the girls in the soap is really into shiatsu, and she's been teaching me all the moves. She says I have great potential—'

'Cassandra.' Jake interrupted her. 'Why did you ring? I can't believe you woke me up to tell me how good you are at some freakin' Japanese massage crap! For God's sake, you left enough messages. I thought there must have been a minor disaster, or something. Instead of which—'

'Mummy's had a stroke,' Cassandra broke in before he could finish, and suddenly every nerve in Jake's body was on high alert. 'It happened on Christmas Eve—can you believe it? I would have told you sooner, but you were away and your mobile was switched off.'

Deliberately, thought Jake grimly. But he was stunned at the news. He could hardly believe that the feisty old lady had suffered a serious attack. She'd seemed so tough, so indomitable. And Eve... How must Eve be feeling? He'd sensed she had real affection for her employer.

'How is she?' he demanded, fully awake now, swinging his bare feet to the floor. 'I assume you've seen her?'

There was silence for a long moment, and Jake was on

the verge of telling her to get a move on when she said, 'Actually, I haven't.'

'You haven't seen her?'

'No,' said Cassandra hurriedly. 'I would have made the trip, you know I would, but she'll be all right. It's not left her paralysed or anything. Eve said she had a bit of, you know, numbness to begin with, but that soon wore off. And it hasn't stopped her from talking—'

Jake blew out a breath. 'I can't believe you haven't been to see her,' he said, aghast. 'Dammit, Cassandra, strokes can be fatal.'

'I know that.' She was defensive now.

'And you didn't think you had a duty to go and see how she was for yourself?' Jake was appalled. 'Cassandra, people need their family around them at a time like this.'

'I know.' Cassandra was sulky. 'But she's got Eve, hasn't she?'

'Eve!' Jake snorted. 'Yeah, that's another story. You didn't think she might appreciate a bit of support, too?'

'Eve doesn't need my support.'

'You mean she's never been offered it.'

Cassandra gasped. 'What do you mean by that? What's she been telling you?'

'Eve hasn't told me anything,' retorted Jake shortly, aware that he had his own faults where Eve was concerned. 'I just think it's a lot to expect of a girl barely out of her teens. Particularly someone whose relationship to your mother is tenuous, to say the least.'

'Oh!' Was that relief in Cassandra's voice? 'Well, you could be right.' She paused. 'But she's not as young as you think, you know. She's twenty-five.'

'She's still a girl,' said Jake flatly. Then, deciding he was in danger of arousing her suspicions again, he said, 'Is Mrs Robertson in Newcastle Hospital?'

'Oh, she's not in hospital,' exclaimed Cassandra at once, as if that somehow exonerated her of much of the blame. 'She's at home.'

'At Watersmeet?'

'Where else?'

'So who's looking after her?'

Cassandra expelled a resentful sigh. 'Well—Eve and Mrs Blackwood, I expect. Eve has been on holiday since it happened.'

'From school, you mean?'

'Of course. You didn't think she'd gone dashing off to some exotic destination as you did?'

'I went home,' Jake reminded her. 'And why shouldn't Eve go on holiday if she wants to? She's entitled to a break, just like anybody else.'

'Not when Mummy's ill,' protested Cassandra brusquely, and then seemed to realise she'd condemned herself out of her own mouth. 'Oh—well, she wouldn't anyway. Eve doesn't do things like that.'

'No.' Jake conceded the point. He had the feeling there were a lot of things Eve didn't do, and he badly wanted to know why.

'Anyway—' Cassandra seemed to think it would be all right to change the subject now '—when am I going to see you?'

You're kidding, right?

For one awful moment Jake thought he'd said the words out loud, but it soon became obvious from Cassandra's anticipation that he hadn't. 'I—' He sought for an answer. 'Let me get back to you on that. Right now I've just got back from San Felipe and I'm pretty tied up.'

'Oh.' Cassandra's response was predictably terse. 'So you don't want to hear my news, then?'

Jake stifled a sigh. 'I thought I just did.'

'No.' Cassandra sniffed. 'I mean *my* news. About my part in *Evermore*.' She paused, evidently waiting for him to respond, and when he didn't she went on resentfully, 'Honestly, I thought you'd be pleased to hear that the preliminary showings—you know, to the press and the executives and so on—have all been positive, and I've been offered a three-month extension of my contract.'

'Great.' Jake wondered how she could consider that more important than her mother's health. 'So you'll be working in London for the foreseeable future?'

'Yes. Marvellous, isn't it? Whenever you're in town, I'll be available.'

I'll just bet you will, thought Jake sourly, not really understanding why her callous attitude should matter so much to him. Okay, so he'd really liked her mother, but so what? He couldn't make himself responsible for Cassandra's shortcomings.

No, the truth was, it was Eve he was concerned about. Eve—who'd been expected to bear the whole weight of the old lady's illness. And it was because of Eve that he was considering how soon he could ditch his schedule and take a flight up to Northumberland.

CHAPTER NINE

IT WAS late when Jake reached Watersmeet. He'd managed to get an afternoon flight, but what with it being an hour late, and the complications of renting a hire car, it was after six when he reached Falconbridge.

There were lights, as before, in the downstairs windows of the house, though this time the curtains were drawn. The arrival of his Ford, which had been all that was on offer, had apparently gone unnoticed, and Jake got out and locked the car before approaching the door.

Once again it was bitterly cold, but this time he was prepared for it. He'd bought himself a cashmere overcoat at Heathrow before boarding the plane, and although he hadn't bothered to fasten it, it was still incredibly warm.

A strange man opened the door to his knock, and Jake gazed at him with wary eyes. Who the hell was this? It couldn't be the Reverend Murray, could it? Had the bastard wheedled his way back into Eve's good graces while Mrs Robertson had been ill? He hoped to God he wasn't here because the old lady had taken a turn for the worse.

'Yes? Can I help you?'

There was such confidence in the man's tone that Jake revised his opinion. Besides, Eve had said Murray was a young man, whereas this guy had to be fifty if he was a day. The doctor, perhaps?

'Er—my name's Romero.' Dammit, this was awkward. He hadn't prepared for this eventuality. 'I'm a friend of—' He could hardly say *the family* so he compromised. 'Of Mrs Robertson's daughter.'

'Yeah? Cass.' The man didn't sound impressed. 'Well, she's not here.'

'I know that—'

'Who is it, Adam?'

Jake heard Eve's voice before he saw her, and he was amazed at the sudden clenching he felt in his gut at the sound. God, he was actually apprehensive of seeing her again, apprehensive of how she'd react when she saw him.

The man—Adam?—half turned at her approach, and because her attention was on him Jake had a moment to absorb her appearance before she noticed him.

She looked tired, he thought at once, the smoky eyes rimmed with dark circles. It was obvious that she hadn't been sleeping well; worried about the old lady, no doubt, unlike Cassandra. Even her hair wasn't neatly plaited, as it had been before. Instead, it was drawn back with a simple ribbon that allowed strands of silky dark hair to stray over the shoulders of the baggy beige cardigan she was wearing.

It made her look younger, he thought, feeling the pull of an attraction that was as insistent as it was out of place. Unlike the cardigan, which had to be a cast-off of the old lady's. It successfully covered her from shoulder to hip, its bulky folds hiding the womanly shape he knew was beneath.

'Jake—Mr Romero!' She'd seen him now, and her eyes had widened in disbelief. 'What are you doing here? Is—?' She looked beyond him. 'Is Cassie with you?'

'No—'

It wasn't the welcome he could have wished for, but it wasn't unexpected. However, before he could explain, the other man intervened. 'You know him?' he asked in some surprise. 'I was just telling him Cassie's not here.'

'I knew that.' Jake had a struggle to keep the edge out

of his voice, but he had no intention of letting this guy screw up his reasons for being here. 'May I come in?'

Eve glanced at the man beside her and then stepped back. 'I expect so,' she said, though there was little enthusiasm in her voice. 'I gather you're on your own. Did Cassie send you?'

'No, she—didn't,' he said, biting back a choice epithet with an effort. He stepped over the threshold, ignoring Adam's grudging stare, and breathed a sigh of relief when the door closed behind him. 'So—how is the old lady?'

Eve looked surprised. 'You know she's been ill?'

Jake sighed. 'Obviously.'

'So Cassie *did* send you?'

'No!'

'But she knows you're here?'

Jake shook his head. 'No to that, too.'

'Then how did you—?'

'I've spoken to Cassandra,' Jake put in levelly. 'That's all.'

Eve looked as if she was having some trouble in taking this in, and Adam seemed to decide that he deserved to know what was going on.

'Who is this chap, Eve?' he asked, giving Jake a suspicious look. 'I thought he said he was a friend of Cassie's?'

'He is.'

Eve couldn't blame him for being confused. She was having a struggle dealing with Jake's arrival herself, and it was difficult to be objective when just seeing him again had thrown all her carefully won indifference into chaos.

He looked so good, she thought, unconsciously pressing a hand to the suddenly hollow place beneath her ribs. In a long camel-coloured overcoat, open over black jeans and a matching sweater, and low-heeled black boots on his feet, he looked even better than she remembered, and she desperately wanted to tell him how glad she was to see him.

But of course she couldn't do that. Apart from the fact that Adam was standing watching him, with a look of wary speculation on his face, Jake was still Cassie's property, not hers.

'So if he's Cassie's—friend—' Jake didn't miss the deliberate emphasis Adam laid on that word '—and he says he knew Cass wasn't here, why the hell has he come?'

'You could start by asking me,' Jake observed pleasantly, even though he itched to make his own contribution to the aggression in the atmosphere. Forcing himself to concentrate on Eve instead, he said, 'How is Mrs Robertson. You didn't say.'

'My mother's fairly fit, considering,' Adam answered for her, and the relief he felt at discovering that Adam wasn't some unknown admirer but Cassandra's brother made Jake feel ridiculously euphoric. 'What's it to you?'

'Adam, you don't understand—'

'I stayed here for a few days last November,' Jake informed him smoothly, overriding Eve's protest. 'With your sister, as it happens. I got to know your mother then. I liked her, and when Cassandra said—'

'Who?'

'Cassandra.' Jake was patient. He'd already realised that her family never used her formal name. 'When she told me her mother had had a stroke, I was concerned.'

'Unlike Cassie,' said Adam tersely. 'That's her real name, by the way. Cassandra's just an affectation she uses when she's acting.'

'Adam—'

Once again Eve tried to intervene, but Adam wasn't having any. 'I still don't get it,' he persisted, glancing sideways at her. 'Is there something going on here that I should know about?'

'No!' Eve's denial was heartfelt, and Jake, who had had no intention of discussing his actions with Adam, guessed that a less arrogant man than himself would have taken that as his cue to get out of there. But he didn't. Giving him a covert look from beneath her lashes, she added, 'Look, why don't we all go into the library? It'll be warmer in there, and we can at least offer Mr Romero a drink, Adam.'

Adam shrugged his bulky shoulders. In appearance he was a lot more like his mother than his sister was, and it was obvious he resented the intrusion of a man he considered little more than Cassandra's—Cassie's—latest admirer. But he didn't argue, which impressed Jake. Evidently Eve's opinion carried more weight in this household than he'd imagined.

And it *was* infinitely warmer in the library. Looking about him, Jake was amazed at how much he remembered of this room, at how familiar it was. And memorable, he thought ruefully. He'd been standing right there when he'd done the unforgivable and kissed Eve. Poor fool that he was, he'd thought he could comfort her. That as soon as he laid his hands on her she'd realise what she'd been missing all along. Yeah, right.

Instead of that she'd stamped on his manhood and his self-respect, and he'd only just got away with saving his dignity.

'Would you like Scotch?'

Eve had moved to the drinks cabinet and was looking at him, and Jake gave her what he hoped was an encouraging smile. 'Great,' he said. Then, remembering he was driving, 'Just a small one, please. Over ice, if you have it.'

Adam snorted. He'd made his way across to the hearth and was now standing warming his back in front of the blazing fire. 'Waste of good whisky, if you ask me,' he muttered. 'Who ruins a good drop of Scotch with ice?'

'I do,' said Jake, determined not to let the other man rile him. 'Do you live in the village, Mr Robertson?'

'No.' Adam's bushy brows drew together above a bulbous nose as he spoke. 'I've got a farm further up the valley. Didn't Cass tell you?'

In actual fact, Cassandra—Cass—had told him very little about her family. Which had suited him very well. But after introducing him to her mother, she might have mentioned that she had a brother in the area, too.

'Did you drive up from London today?'

Eve was speaking, evidently realising that Adam was bent on being objectionable and trying to keep the peace.

'No. I took a flight to Newcastle,' Jake answered easily. 'I rented a car at the airport.'

'To come here?' said Adam unpleasantly. 'How sweet.'

Jake wondered if the man had a death wish. Right now he was having a hard time keeping his temper with the evidence of Eve's exhaustion there in front of his eyes. Did this guy have any conception that she appeared to be bearing the whole burden of the old lady's illness? What contribution had *he* made, apart from behaving like the ignorant lout he was?

'Ellie will be pleased to see you,' said Eve hurriedly, once again trying to lighten the mood. 'She's been virtually confined to her room since her illness. She'll be delighted to see a fresh face.'

'And such a pretty face,' said Adam sarcastically, clearly under the impression that Jake wouldn't—or couldn't—retaliate.

But this time Jake had had enough. 'Have you got a

problem with me being here?' he demanded, ignoring Eve's automatic attempt to come between them. 'Stay out of this,' he advised her, keeping his attention focussed on the other man. 'Well? Have you?'

Adam blustered. 'That's not the point.'

'Then what is?' Jake was intimidating in this mood, and Eve realised her uncle had definitely underestimated him. 'As I understand it, you don't own this house. So you don't have any say over who comes or goes, right?'

Adam was clearly agitated, but he stood his ground. 'Well, *she* doesn't,' he snorted, gesturing towards Eve. 'It's not her house, either.'

Which was a perfectly pointless thing to say, in Jake's opinion. Dammit, he knew it wasn't Eve's house. She only worked here. Despite what Cassandra had said about her being a distant relative, she was obviously treated more like a housemaid than a member of the family.

'He knows that, Adam,' Eve protested, putting a glass into Jake's hand now, as if that would prevent him from shoving his fist in the other man's fleshy face. 'For goodness' sake, what's wrong with you? Mr Romero's a guest, not an intruder. And, whether you like it or not, Ellie likes him.'

Adam grunted. 'If you say so.'

'I do say so.' Eve gave him a glass, too. 'Now, drink your drink and stop behaving like an idiot.'

'Who are you calling an idiot?' Adam was indignant, but Jake was amazed to see a reluctant smile tugging at the corners of his mouth. He gave a Jake a grudging look and then added gruffly, 'Sorry. But Cass's admirers usually rub me up the wrong way.'

Jake was taken aback. He'd never expected the man to apologise, and he supposed he should feel grateful to Eve for rescuing the situation. But he didn't. He was put out now, and he badly wanted to take his frustration out on someone.

Speaking between his teeth, he said, 'I guess this has been a rough time for both of you. Eve certainly looks as if she's borne the brunt of it.'

'Jake!'

Eve used his name without thinking, but he barely had time to register his approval before Adam said, 'I've got a farm to run, Mr Romero. A hundred and fifty acres and two hundred head of cattle that need milking twice a day. Doesn't leave me much time for anything else.'

'Then perhaps you ought to have thought of employing an agency nurse to look after your mother?' retorted Jake, swallowing half his Scotch in one gulp. 'Eve's not a servant, you know.'

'I know that.' Adam's voice rose an octave, but then he seemed to think better of tangling with the younger man. 'Anyway, what's it to you? Eve's big enough to make her own complaints if she wants to.'

'For goodness' sake!' It was Eve who spoke. 'Will you two stop behaving as if I wasn't here? I was quite happy to look after Ellie, Mr Romero. And Adam would have hired a nurse if I'd asked him to. As it is, he's going to take her to recuperate at the farm for a couple of weeks, so I can have a rest. Okay?'

Jake's jaw compressed. 'Is that true?'

'What? That Ellie's going to the farm for a couple of weeks?' Eve sighed. 'Yes, it is, as it happens. Adam's wife used to be a nurse, so she's quite capable of looking after her. Satisfied?'

He blew out a breath. 'I guess so.'

'Good.'

Eve sipped at the diet cola she'd poured for herself and hoped her words had defused the situation. Her earlier excitement at seeing Jake again had been dissipated by the atmosphere he and Adam had created, but that was probably just as well. Nevertheless, she was left with the uneasy awareness that she had let her feelings blind her to the real dangers here. She didn't honestly know why Jake had come. She could only take his words about her grandmother at face value. But she knew that whatever he said, whatever he wanted of her, she couldn't allow a momentary madness to develop into something even more destructive.

'Look, I'm going up to say goodbye to my mother before I leave,' Adam said suddenly, crossing the room to deposit his empty glass on the tray. He turned to Jake. 'Why don't you come up and see her? As Eve says, she'll probably be glad to have someone different to talk to.'

Jake only hesitated a moment. Despite the fact that he'd been waiting for Adam to leave so that he could speak to Eve alone, he couldn't ignore the olive branch the other man was extending.

'Thanks,' he said stiffly. 'I'd like that.'

When they'd gone, Eve breathed a sigh of relief. For a moment there she'd thought Jake was going to refuse—and how could she have explained that to her uncle? As it was, she just hoped their armistice would last as long as it took to visit Ellie and convince her that Jake's only reason for coming here had been to assure himself that she'd suffered no ill effects from the attack.

And it was probably true, Eve thought, gathering the dirty glasses onto a tray and carrying it to the door. After all, it was hardly flattering to know that the main thing he'd noticed about her was how tired she looked. As compared to Cassie, she assumed, her lips tightening with sudden pain. So what was new?

Jake hadn't come down when she returned to the library, and, unwilling to sit there waiting for him, Eve decided to go out to the stables. She knew Storm Dancer would already be safe in her stall. Mick, the man Mr Trivett employed to do all the odd jobs around the estate, would have seen to that. But she always gained a certain amount of comfort from the mare's company, and hopefully Jake would get the message and leave before she got back.

Storm Dancer was munching happily from her feed bag when Eve rested her folded arms along the rails of her stall. The mare looked up, but she didn't come to greet her, and Eve guessed that even the promise of an apple wouldn't distract her from her food.

'Your loss, old girl,' Eve said, and with a rueful smile she glanced behind her. There was a neat stack of straw bales piled against the wall opposite, and she pulled a couple down to make a seat.

Watching the mare was almost as soothing to her ruffled nerves as grooming her would be, and, propping her elbows on her knees, Eve cupped her chin in her hands.

She guessed she must have been sitting there for fifteen minutes when she became aware that she was no longer alone. Jake was leaning with folded arms against the empty stall next to Storm Dancer's. His booted feet were crossed at the ankle and there was a disturbingly intent look on his lean, dark face.

The fact that he'd entered the stables without her hearing him caused her no small measure of unease. Her thoughts had obviously been miles away, and anyone could have come into the isolated building and surprised her.

'Hi,' he said, when she looked up and saw him, and a quiver of awareness stirred in her belly. But when she would have got to her feet, he waved her back. 'Stay where you are,' he said, straightening from the rail and coming towards her. 'I'll join you. This is as good a place as any to talk.'

Eve shifted a little uncertainly. 'I ought to be getting back.'

'Why?'

Why indeed?

'I'm cold,' she said, the facile excuse the first that occurred to her. 'I've been sitting here too long.'

'Don't I know it?' Jake seated himself on the bale beside her and took off his coat, draping its soft folds about her shoulders. It was still warm from his body, still smelled of his distinctive scent. The beautiful garment trailed carelessly on the stable floor, but he didn't seem to notice. 'I've been waiting for you to come back.'

Eve shivered, but not with the cold. 'How did you know where I was?'

'Mrs Blackwood said I'd probably find you here,' he replied, his breath warm against her cheek. 'She gave me strict instructions on how to find you.' His eyes dropped to her mouth. 'I didn't like to tell her I already knew.'

Eve's breathing quickened. 'I thought you'd leave as soon as you'd spoken to Ellie. After the way Adam treated you, I'd have expected you'd want to get as far from here as possible.'

'You wish?' he murmured, his voice low and vaguely suggestive, awakening all those unfamiliar feelings inside her again. 'Is that why you've been sitting out here? Because you were hoping to avoid seeing me again.'

Yes!

'No.' Eve thought she sounded at least half convincing. 'Why should you think that?'

His mouth compressed. 'You know why.' He paused.

'I suppose I should apologise. I had no right to try and kiss you.'

Eve's throat felt tight with suppressed emotion. 'I shouldn't have reacted as I did,' she said. Then, with a nervous sideways glance, 'Did I hurt you?'

His mouth twitched. 'If I said you did, what would you do about it? Kiss it better?'

Eve's face flamed, but when she would have got to her feet Jake's hand on her knee prevented her. 'I'm sorry,' he said ruefully. 'I shouldn't have said that. Will you forgive me?'

He could feel her knee trembling beneath his hand, and he cursed himself for a fool. He'd already guessed that at some time some man had hurt her badly, and if he wanted to see her again he had to stop crowding her.

'Look,' he said, resisting the urge to slide his hand further up her thigh, 'can't we put the past behind us and start again?'

Eve's lips parted. 'There's nothing to start again, Mr Romero!' she exclaimed, and Jake thought he could willingly drown in the limpid beauty of her eyes. 'I think you're getting me mixed up with Cassandra.'

'No, I'm not.' Jake disliked the sound of that woman's name on her lips. 'I've thought of little else but you ever since I left here.'

Eve tensed. 'You're joking, right?'

'It's the truth.'

'Oh, right.' She was sceptical. 'So I'm supposed to believe that all the time you were making love to Cassandra you were really thinking of me? How sick is that?'

'I haven't had sex with Cassandra,' he snapped, resenting her sarcasm. He made an impatient gesture. 'What kind of a creep do you think I am?'

'I don't have an opinion, Mr Romero,' she replied

primly, irritating him anew with her refusal to use his given name. 'I hardly know you.'

'We could remedy that.' Despite his intention to move slowly, Jake allowed his fingers to stroke the inner curve of her knee. A nerve jumped against his hand and he felt the immediate quiver of apprehension that rippled over her at his touch. 'I want to.'

'Well, I don't,' said Eve, but her mouth was dry and she knew it wasn't quite the truth. His nearness was having a totally unprecedented effect on her senses, and although she wanted to dislodge his hand from her knee, curiosity—and an undeniable temptation—kept her from doing it.

'Don't you?' He leant closer and she felt his tongue stroke her ear. 'Are you sure about that?'

'Jake!' His name was a cry of protest, but when she turned her head to avoid his tongue she found his face only inches from hers.

And something shifted deep inside her—something that kept her staring at him when she knew she shouldn't be doing this, shouldn't be as close as this to any man, and particularly not this man.

His eyes were dark, and dilated to such an extent that she could hardly see any whiteness at all. And, although she was sure he must have shaved that morning, already there was a shadow of stubble on his jawline.

He had such a beautiful face, she thought, which was a crazy thought to have about someone who was so essentially male. But his was a hard beauty, his eyes deep, his mouth thin yet so sinfully sensual that any woman would be entranced.

A fine tremor ran though her which must have communicated itself to him, because he lifted his hand and allowed his knuckles to graze her cheek.

The tremor became an earthquake, and Eve felt her resistance ebbing as the shaking in her shoulders spread to the rest of her body. Her breathing was shallow, yet she could hear her heart pounding in her ears. She was transfixed. Yet how could that be when inside she felt as if a series of electrical explosions was tearing her apart?

His thumb moved to brush roughly across her lips and her tongue went instinctively to meet it. He tasted as good as he looked, she thought, and, as if sensing her submission, he pressed harder, causing her lips to part. And, God forgive her, she curled her tongue around him and sucked his thumb into her mouth.

She heard the catch of his breathing, the quickening of the pulse that beat against her tongue. He was watching her with a heavy-lidded intensity that even she knew was different than before, and the feelings inside her expanded to consume every part of her being.

She needed to touch him, and her hands rose almost jerkily to grasp the soft fabric of his sweater, as if by holding on to him she could control this madness inside. Beneath the wool, the heat of his skin rose to meet her clutching fingers, and she desperately wanted to burrow beneath his sweater and press herself against the hard flesh of his body.

'God, I want you,' he said, his voice hoarse and unsteady, and Eve could only gaze up at him, unconsciously inviting him to go on.

His hand settled at the back of her neck, under the soft mane of her hair, his touch warm and heavy, angling her head to his. His kiss when it came was different, too, hard and deliberate, taking as well as giving, as if he was afraid she was going to run out on him again before it was over.

But she didn't. She couldn't. The fire of that kiss had

burned away any resistance, igniting a path clear down to her groin so that her legs fell helplessly apart.

She didn't realise that Storm Dancer had finished feeding and was now standing watching them with soft, uncritical eyes. She was barely conscious of anything but Jake's needs, Jake's heat, the hungry pressure of his tongue forcing its way into her mouth.

He kissed her many times, over and over, until she was weak and clinging to him. He urged her back against the straw bales behind her and her breasts ached with the pressure he was putting on them, but she didn't care. He'd wedged one thigh between hers, so that there was no way she could avoid feeling his arousal. His shaft throbbed against her leg and she shuddered with the awareness of how big he was, how hard and male and virile—and dangerously out of control.

'Do you have any idea how long I've wanted to do this?' he demanded thickly, releasing her mouth only to nip her earlobe, to bite the yielding flesh of her throat. 'I knew you'd be beautiful and you are.'

'I'm—not —beautiful,' she protested unsteadily, but he wasn't listening to her. He'd parted the heavy cardigan to expose the thin vest that was all she was wearing underneath. He seemed entranced by the swollen globes of her breasts and, pushing the vest aside, his cold hands sought and released the catch of her bra

Eve's head swam when her breasts spilled into his hands. His thumbs had found the sensitised peaks that had surged against his palms, and she ached now with needs of her own. There was a tingling in her stomach and a throbbing wetness between her legs that she'd definitely never felt before. She felt alive and desirable, and, clutching his face with both hands, she brought his mouth back to hers.

'Easy, baby,' he murmured against her lips, and Eve trembled. How could she take it easy when it was all so new, so exciting, so different from anything she'd ever experienced before? His tongue was making sensuous forays into her mouth, aping what he wanted to do to her body, and for the first time she faced the possibility of a man's lovemaking without fear or disgust.

'We've got all night,' he whispered, easing her back until she was practically lying on the bales, his hand sliding down to cup her mound through the tight cotton of her jeans. 'No one's going to interrupt us.'

No one, mused Eve dizzily. No one—not even Cassie. Cassie...

Eve's throat constricted. The thought was a chilling one. It reminded her of who Jake was, how she had met him. Dear God, what was she thinking, allowing this to happen? Was she so bemused by her own discovered sexuality that she was prepared to make love to a man who, by his own admission, was still seeing the other woman? A man who, by every law of decency, was forbidden to her?

He had bent his head and was about to take one engorged nipple into his mouth when Eve uttered a strangled denial. 'No,' she said, a very real panic giving her voice the edge of hysteria. 'No. No, you can't. You don't understand.' Wriggling out from under him, she hurriedly pulled the folds of her cardigan together and faced him with wide, agonised eyes. 'We can't do this. I can't do this. It wouldn't be right.'

Jake stared at her. Despite the fact that he was very obviously aroused, and his expression mirrored the frustration he was feeling, his voice was unnaturally quiet when he said, 'This is about Cassandra, isn't it? You think that because Cassandra introduced us—'

'No. No, it's not that.'

Eve moved her head frantically from side to side, but Jake's patience wasn't infinite. 'What, then?' he asked, his voice hardening a little. 'I've told you I'm not interested in Cassandra. Okay, so I know she's a relative of yours, but that can't be helped. She'll get over it.'

'No! No, she won't.'

The panic was rising in Eve's voice now, and Jake seemed to realise there was more than simple anxiety about a distant cousin going on here. 'What, then?' he said again, controlling his temper with an obvious effort. 'Why do we need to concern ourselves with what she thinks? She's not your keeper, is she?'

'She's my mother,' said Eve, her chest heaving with emotion. 'Now do you see why I can't have anything more to do with you? She's my *mother*!'

CHAPTER TEN

JAKE drove back to London in the foulest of moods. He left without seeing Eve again, driving through the night, arriving back at his hotel in the early hours of the morning.

He knew he'd have some kind of penalty to pay for bringing the rental car back to London, but financial concerns weren't of much interest to him in his present state of mind. He was angry—and gutted. He couldn't believe he'd been crazy enough to fall for Cassandra's *daughter*. Cassandra's daughter, for God's sake! No wonder there was no love lost between the two of them.

Or between Cassandra and her mother, he appended, remembering the conversation he'd had with the old lady before he left. For pity's sake, what kind of monster had he been dealing with? What kind of woman abandoned her kid without even telling her own mother that she'd had a child?

He'd got the story from the old lady, of course. Eve hadn't told him anything. After delivering her bombshell, she hadn't hung around to answer any questions. Even though he'd insisted that she couldn't say something like that without making some form of explanation, she'd refused to offer any excuses for her behaviour.

Like why she hadn't told him she was Cassandra's daughter before now. Oh, he wasn't a fool. Not a complete one, he hoped. It was obvious Cassandra had never acknowledged her daughter, and for some reason Eve was prepared to go along with that; to the extent that she'd let him think she was only there through Mrs Robertson's good graces.

Mrs Robertson! Jake ground his teeth together. Dammit, the woman Eve called Ellie was her *grandmother*! Whose idea had it been to hide their relationship? Surely not the old lady's? Without her intervention, Eve—

But he refused to think about that now. Not when there was nothing he could do about it. But as soon as it was light he intended to go and see Cassandra, and have her version of the story. There was no way he could put this to bed without hearing the truth from her.

The words he'd used mocked him. How the hell was he going to 'put this to bed', whatever Cassandra said? His feelings for Eve weren't going to go away that easily, if at all. No matter how often he reminded himself that she'd deceived him just as much as her mother had, he couldn't get her out of his mind.

He wanted her. No. More than that. He wanted to be with her. He wanted to take her in his arms and finish what they'd started a few hours ago—in the stables, of all places. And the knowledge that she'd spurned him was tearing him apart.

Yet he mustn't forget she was Cassandra's daughter. And how could any daughter of that woman ever be anything but trouble? If he had any sense he'd be grateful he'd found out in time, before he'd done something irrevocable. Like making love to her, for example. He had the feeling that if he'd ever possessed her body, if he'd ever found his release with her, there would have been no way for him to escape his demons.

He felt raw, he thought bitterly. Raw and frustrated. Desperate to make someone else suffer as he was suffering now. It was a new experience for him, and one he had no intention of allowing to happen again.

It was still barely three o'clock in the morning, and despite the adrenalin in his system that had enabled him to drive almost three hundred miles without even a break he was exhausted. He had to remember he'd hardly slept the night before, and although the time change between here and San Felipe had given him a little breathing space, his own limitations were catching up with him.

He needed to rest, and, stripping off his clothes, he crawled into bed without even taking a shower. He wanted nothing to refresh him, nothing to get his mind working again. But although he closed his eyes he remained wide awake.

The image of Eve's face as he'd last seen her drifted between him and the nirvana he sought. He could still taste her on his tongue, still smell her womanly fragrance on his hands, still feel her hands reaching for him, her mouth opening for his hungry invasion...

God! He groaned, rolling over and burying his hot face in the pillow. No matter who she was, no matter how she'd treated him, he still wanted her. The hard-on he had just wasn't going to go away, and he knew if he was ever going to get any sleep he would have to do something about it himself.

It didn't work. Not immediately, anyway. He just felt cold, and disgusted with himself for letting it happen. But eventually sleep overwhelmed him, and when he opened his eyes again it was daylight.

He ordered coffee and toast from Room Service, and then took a shower in the time it took for his breakfast to be delivered.

With several doses of caffeine and a couple of slices of toast filling the empty space inside him, he felt a little better. After dressing, he went downstairs and arranged with the concierge for the Ford to be delivered to wherever the rental company wanted, and then left the hotel.

It was still only a little after nine o'clock, and he'd expected Cassandra would be at the studios. However, after ringing her number and ascertaining she was still at her apartment, he summoned a taxi and gave the man her address.

He hadn't spoken to her. He'd hung up as soon as he'd heard her voice. He wanted to see her face when he confronted her with her duplicity; he wanted to be there when she tried to explain why she'd sold her own daughter to strangers as soon as she was born.

Cassandra lived in Notting Hill. She occupied half the top floor of a converted Victorian terrace house, and although Jake had never been into the place, he'd delivered her home a couple of times so he knew where it was.

His initial ring on the bell that served her apartment elicited no response. But, as luck would have it, one of the other tenants emerged as he was standing there, and he managed to save the door from closing and slip inside.

Postboxes in the hall gave him the number of her apartment, and Jake climbed swiftly to the second floor. He hoped she hadn't gone out in the time it had taken him to get here. Traffic in London was always hectic, whatever the time of day, and this morning was no exception.

Cassandra opened the door at his third ring. She'd obviously just got out of bed, and Jake recognised the familiar red kimono she'd wrapped about her naked body. He knew she'd be able to tell from his expression that this wasn't a social call, but he was surprised when she glanced guiltily over her shoulder before edging the door almost closed again.

'Jake!' she exclaimed in a low voice. 'What are you doing here?'

Almost the same words her daughter had used the evening before, thought Jake cynically. Well, it served him right for not warning her he was coming. Particularly as it seemed she wasn't alone.

'We need to talk,' he said flatly. 'Can I come in?'

Once again there was that nervous peep over her shoulder. 'We can't talk now,' she said, looking back at him. 'Darling, I didn't get to bed until after two, and I'm beat. There was a party at the studios, you see, and—'

'I'm not interested in where you've been or who you've been with,' said Jake, pressing one hand against the panels and propelling the door open. 'We're going to talk, Cassandra—or should I say *Cassie*? That is what your daughter calls you, isn't it?'

Cassandra's mouth fell open, and for a moment she did nothing to stop his advance into the apartment. But then she seemed to come to her senses and made a futile attempt to obstruct him. 'You can't come in here now,' she said. 'I—I'm not alone.'

'Do I look like I care?' Jake moved her aside with the minimum amount of effort and glanced round what was probably the main room of the apartment. Running from the front to the back of the building, it appeared to be half-kitchen, half-living-cum-dining-area. And, typical of Cassandra, it was grossly untidy, with articles of clothing and magazines strewn haphazardly across the floor.

'You have no right to force your way in here,' she exclaimed, bending to pick up what looked like a man's shirt and stuffing it behind one of the cushions on the sofa. 'This isn't funny, Jake. I don't barge into your hotel suite without an invitation, and you should do the same.'

'Oh, I've been invited here many times,' said Jake carelessly. 'So let's pretend I'm just taking you up on it.'

'Let's not.' Cassandra cast another nervous glance towards what could only be the door into her bedroom. 'I don't want you here.'

'Too bad, because you've got me.' Flinging himself onto the sofa, he linked his hands behind his head and crossed his feet at the ankles. 'Now, isn't this cosy?'

Cassandra seethed. 'What do you want, Jake?'

'Ah, that's better.' He was complacent. 'So, why don't you sit down and I'll tell you?'

She took a deep breath. 'I don't want to sit down.' Another glance at the bedroom. 'I don't have time to sit. I have to be at the studios in an hour.'

'That should be enough time.' Jake regarded her through his dark lashes. 'So, tell me about your daughter.'

Cassandra swallowed. 'I don't have a daughter.'

'Liar.'

Cassandra scowled at him. 'I don't know where you've got this preposterous story from, but—'

'Try your daughter.'

'Eve *told* you?'

Jake's expression hardened. 'Did I say her name was Eve?' he queried coldly, and Cassandra turned away to fuss with a pair of stockings that were draped over the arm of a chair.

'Well, who else could have told you such a ridiculous story?' she demanded, purposefully avoiding his eyes as she spoke.

'How about your mother?'

'My mother?' Cassandra did turn then. 'Oh, Jake, you know what that old witch thinks of me. How can you believe anything she says?'

Jake's gaze was intent. 'So it's not true?'

'No.' But her eyes shifted past him as she spoke. 'No, of course it's not true. Good heavens, Eve's—what?

Twenty-five? I'd have had to be an adolescent when I had her.'

'Your mother says you're forty-six,' said Jake bluntly. 'Quite old enough to have a twenty-five-year-old daughter.'

Cassandra gasped. 'I'm not forty-six!'

'No?'

'No.'

Jake sat up then, spreading his legs and resting his forearms along his thighs. 'So the birth certificate your mother showed me is a forgery?'

Cassandra stared at him. 'What birth certificate? How can you have seen a birth certificate?' She paused. 'Are you telling me you've been to Watersmeet? Without asking me?'

'I didn't know I needed your permission to visit a sick old lady,' said Jake harshly, pressing his hands down on his knees and getting to his feet. 'So? Is it a forgery?'

Cassandra hesitated. 'Whose—whose birth certificate have you seen?'

Jake shook his head. 'Well, not yours,' he said scathingly. 'But perhaps you could explain how a—let me see—how a thirteen-year-old girl, such as yourself, was pretending to be a twenty-year-old living and working in London at the time Eve was born?'

Cassandra's shoulders sagged. 'I don't see that it's anything to do with you,' she said bitterly. 'I think you'd better go.'

'Oh, not yet.' Jake's eyes were hard. 'I want to hear the story from your lips. I want to know how you could abandon your daughter to the care of people you knew virtually nothing about?'

'I didn't abandon her,' said Cassandra defensively, clearly deciding there was no point in continuing to lie.

'The Fultons were very good to me, actually. If it hadn't been for them I'd have been out on the street.'

'But you didn't know them. Not really,' said Jake harshly. 'You'd met them in a pub, for God's sake!'

'Yes, well...' Cassandra struggled for words. 'I could have had an abortion, you know.'

'But they persuaded you not to?'

'I was upset. They said they'd help me.'

Jake's contempt was palpable. 'Where was the baby's father?'

'Oh, he didn't want to know,' said Cassandra at once, wrapping the kimono closer about her. 'After—after I discovered I was pregnant, I never saw him again.'

Jake looked sceptical. 'Did you ever tell him you were having a baby?'

'Of course.' Cassandra huffed. 'As I say, he didn't want to know.'

'According to the enquiries your mother made after she discovered she had a granddaughter, you told the registrar you didn't know who the child's father was.'

Cassandra's face blazed with colour. 'What else could I do? I had to say something.'

'Why didn't you tell your mother you were pregnant?'

'You're joking!' Cassandra stared at him. 'Can you imagine what would have happened if I had?'

'She says she would have been quite happy for you to come home and have the baby.'

'Oh, right.' Cassandra was contemptuous. 'I'd spent half my life wanting to get out of Falconbridge. Do you really think I'd have given up everything I'd worked for the past four years to go back there because I'd been stupid enough to get myself pregnant? No, thanks.'

'You didn't even tell your mother about the baby!'

'No.' Cassandra nodded. 'How could I? She'd have insisted on me keeping it.'

'And would that have been so bad?'

'Are you kidding? We're not talking about the way things are today, Jake. Twenty-five years ago single mothers had a pretty tough time, socially and financially.'

'So you sold your baby?'

'I—I didn't exactly sell her.'

'No? What would you call it?'

'After Eve was born, the Fultons came to the poky bed-sit where I was living and suggested that they could look after her. They'd been trying for years to have a baby of their own, but it just wasn't happening. They said they'd give her a good home and—and give me a certain sum of money, if I agreed to let them keep her.'

'So you sold her?'

'If you insist on being pedantic, all right. I sold her.'

'To a man who tried to abuse her when she was twelve years old.'

Cassandra sniffed. 'We only have Eve's word for that.'

'She ran away. Three times. She told me that.'

'So?' Cassandra turned away. 'Lots of kids run away from home.'

'The authorities must have believed her eventually. She was put into care, wasn't she?'

'She was uncontrollable.'

Jake wanted to hurt her, badly, but he kept his temper with an effort. 'Whatever—she spent the next three years with Social Services.'

'Until she ran away again, with some boy she'd taken up with,' Cassandra put in spitefully. 'When my mother found them they were living in a squat in Islington.'

'So your mother said,' said Jake, amazed that his voice

sounded so unthreatening. 'I'm interested to know how the old lady came to find out she had a granddaughter.'

'Didn't she tell you that, too?'

'Oh, yes, she told me. I'd just like to hear your take on it. As I understand it, you weren't averse to returning home when you thought you were dying.'

'That's a cruel thing to say.' Cassandra cast another apprehensive glance towards the bedroom door, almost as if she was more afraid of her visitor finding out that she'd once been diagnosed with a potentially terminal kidney disease than the fact that she'd sold her baby. 'I—I needed help.'

'Yeah, you needed help all right.' Jake spoke contemptuously. 'You needed a transplant. And because you were afraid your mother's kidney might not be good enough you had to tell her that you'd once given birth to a child, but that you didn't know where that child was, right?'

'Why ask me? You seem to know all the answers.'

'Yeah.' Jake felt sick. There was no remorse in Cassandra's tone at all. 'But your mother's kidney *was* good enough, wasn't it? You must have been kicking yourself when you found out you'd made your confession for nothing.' He made a helpless gesture. 'I don't know how you live with yourself.'

Cassandra's lips tightened. 'So? What are you going to do about it?'

'What am *I* going to do about it?'

'That's what I said.' Cassandra's face mirrored the uncertainty she was feeling. 'You're not going to tell anyone else, are you?'

'Who else?' Jake was scornful. 'Who would be interested?'

Cassandra shrugged, but she still looked wary. 'Nobody, I suppose.'

'Oh, I get it.' Jake had caught on. 'You're afraid I might give this to the tabloid press, aren't you? Well, don't worry, Cassandra. I won't tell anyone your dirty little secret. You're not the only person who's involved here.'

Cassandra stared at him. Then she uttered a scornful sound. 'Of course. I should have known. It wasn't concern for my mother that took you up to Northumberland, was it? It was Eve. My sainted daughter.' She gave a harsh laugh. 'My God, you're no better than me.'

'Oh, I am. Believe me, I am.' Jake couldn't control his anger now, and Cassandra hurriedly put the width of the sofa between them. 'As far as Eve is concerned, you're her mother, and that makes any relationship between us taboo.' He scowled. 'But you know what? That's okay. I don't need another woman like you in my life.'

CHAPTER ELEVEN

THE aircraft began its decent into San Felipe in the late afternoon, local time. She had been flying for hours and hours, first in a huge jet and then in this small turboprop, and Eve, who hadn't yet set her watch for San Felipe time, saw it was already after nine o'clock back in England. But she wasn't tired. She was too excited for that. Excited, but apprehensive, too. This was such a big step, and, while her grandmother had urged her to take it, she couldn't help the uneasy thought that Jake wouldn't really be glad to see her.

So much had happened in such a short time, and she was still reeling from her grandmother's decision to sell Watersmeet Hall. But the old lady had decided she was getting too old to stay there with only Mrs Blackwood for company when Eve was at work. And, as it seemed that if Eve wanted to continue teaching she would have to get a job in Newcastle, Ellie had decided to accept Adam's invitation and live with them.

Mrs Blackwood didn't mind. She was elderly herself, and had been thinking of retiring for some time. Only Eve presented a problem, and, although Adam had offered her a home too, Eve had decided to get a place of her own.

And that was when the letter from the school authorities in San Felipe had arrived. Apparently, there was a small school on the island, and they needed a teacher. They'd be happy to offer the position to Eve, they'd said, with a two-months probationary period on both sides. If it didn't work out, Eve would be given a return ticket to England.

She'd known at once that Jake had to be behind the offer. What she couldn't understand was why he would feel the need to do such a thing. She'd been left in no doubt about his reaction when he'd discovered Cassie was her mother, and she hadn't been surprised that she hadn't heard from him since.

Her grandmother hadn't hesitated in urging her to take the job, however, at least for the probationary period. 'What have you got to lose?' she'd demanded, when Eve had expressed her doubts to her. 'Just because he was foolish enough to get involved with Cassie doesn't make him a bad person. He obviously liked you, and when I told him you were losing your job at Easter he must have wondered if you'd like a change of scene.'

'When did you tell him I was losing my job at Easter?' Eve had asked warily, but for once her grandmother had been unusually vague.

'Does it matter?' she'd protested. 'This is a wonderful opportunity, Eve. You deserve it. And if you don't like living in the West Indies you can always come home.'

Which was true, Eve thought now, as the misgivings she'd had ever since she'd written and accepted the offer asserted themselves again. She was afraid what she was really doing was just building up more misery for herself in the months to come.

Naturally, Cassie hadn't approved of the idea. When Ellie had rung her daughter to tell her where Eve was going she had been at pains to remind Eve—via her grandmother—that Jake couldn't be trusted. He'd apparently visited Cassie again, before he left for San Felipe, and Eve got the impression that their affair was by no means over.

Of course she'd told no one what had happened in the stables the evening Jake had arrived to see her grandmother. Indeed, there'd been times since then when she'd wondered if she'd just imagined the whole thing. But then she'd wake in the morning with her pillow clasped in her arms and drenched with tears, and she'd know that no fantasy could have created such physical despair.

She wondered if Ellie would have been so keen to send her off to San Felipe if she'd known what had happened. If she'd known how Eve really felt about Jake. Eve doubted it. As far as the old lady was concerned this was an unexpected solution to all their problems, and Eve hadn't had the heart to tell her how she really felt.

Yet how *did* she really feel? Eve wondered now, as the shape of San Felipe solidified below them. Wasn't she secretly looking forward to seeing Jake again, whatever happened? You couldn't care about someone and not care if you never saw them again. However impossible any relationship between them might be, she still wanted to see him, to show him, if nothing else, that she was nothing like her mother.

The plane flew in over white roofs and rich green vegetation, with the white sandy beaches and deep blue waters of the Caribbean framing the exotic picture. There was no airport as such, just a cluster of colour-washed buildings surrounded by a metal fence, with what might have been a barn—or a hangar—at the end of the short runway.

'This is it, folks.'

The flight attendant, a young man dressed in an open-necked white shirt and black pants, got up from his seat before the plane had taxied to a halt and began dragging hand luggage from a locker set at the front of the plane. Apart from himself and the pilot there were no other attendants, but that was okay. There were only a dozen passengers on the flight.

The plane stopped, the door was opened, and Eve joined her fellow passengers as they got up to disembark. A flight of steps had been pushed up against the door, and although she'd earlier experienced the intense heat of the islands in Grand Cayman, it hit her again as she stepped down onto the hot tarmac.

'Have a good holiday,' said the grinning attendant, and Eve didn't bother to correct him.

'Thanks,' she said, her eyes already searching the group of people waiting at the gate. But there was no one there she knew, and she looped her haversack over her shoulder and pushed through into the excuse for a customs hall.

Seconds later she'd had her passport checked, and was waiting to collect her luggage when a hand touched her bare arm. 'You must be Miss Robertson,' said a soft, attractive voice, and she turned to find a slim, dark-skinned young woman standing beside her.

'I—yes,' she said, dropping the heavy haversack on to the floor with some relief. 'Hello.'

'Hello,' responded the woman, her smile warm and friendly. 'Jake asked me to meet you. I'm Isabel Rodrigues.'

'Miss Rodrigues!' Eve was taken aback. She knew from the letter she'd had from the education authorities in San Felipe that the head teacher at the school was called Rodrigues. But she'd never expected anyone like this— as young as this. A vision of Mrs Portman intruded— middle-aged and portly, with greying hair and horn-rimmed spectacles. Isabel Rodrigues was beautiful, and Eve couldn't help wondering exactly how well she knew Jake Romero. 'Um—it was good of you to come and meet me.'

'No problem.' Isabel's voice had a musical quality to it. 'Did you have a good journey?'

'A long journey,' said Eve wryly. 'But, yes, it was good. Interesting. I've never made such a long journey before.'

'So you've never been to the islands before?'

'No.' Eve refrained from saying that most teachers didn't have the funds to holiday in the West Indies. 'I've never been that fortunate.'

'Hmm.' Isabel nodded. 'Well, I'm sure you won't find it difficult to get used to. The heat may be a problem to begin with, but we start school fairly early in the morning and finish at lunchtime, so you won't be required to work at the hottest time of the day.'

'That's good.' Eve fanned herself with a nervous hand. 'It is rather enervating, isn't it?'

'Not to me,' Isabel assured her, as a trolley containing the luggage from the small plane was wheeled into the area. 'How many cases do you have?'

'Oh—only one,' said Eve ruefully, guessing that Isabel Rodrigues would never dream of travelling with only one suitcase. Her slim-fitting slip dress was simple enough, but made of silk, its colours a vibrant blend of orange and yellow that complemented her dark colouring.

Eve, herself, felt out of place in her jeans and tee shirt, despite the fact that she'd shed the leather jacket her grandmother had given her as a going-away present in Grand Cayman. But it had still been a cool March when she'd left London, and nothing could have prepared her for this heat. Even her hair felt like a heavy weight, weighing her head down, and for the first time in years she toyed with the idea of having it cut to a more manageable length.

A few minutes later, with a porter towing Eve's suitcase, her haversack draped about his neck, they emerged into the sunlight. A handful of taxis waited outside the building, but Isabel led the way to where an open-topped Mazda was waiting for them.

'This is it,' she said, with obvious pride, and although Eve had hoped for a saloon, she duly admired the sleek red convertible.

With the luggage stowed in the back, Isabel directed Eve to get into the car. Luckily, she'd spread a light rug over the seats, so that the leather didn't burn their legs. Then, after sliding behind the wheel, she took off.

Eve realised at once that the car being open to the air was no problem. Isabel drove fast, and the breeze off the ocean was cool and delicious in her face. It enabled her to enjoy the fantastic views of deserted beaches lapped by pale green waters edged with foam. Inland, forested gullies rose towards the centre of the island, the thick vegetation liberally interspersed with blooms of dazzling colour. It was all so different, so exotic, and Eve forgot her apprehension in the sheer delight of being here.

'The island's not very big,' Isabel confided as they passed through a small fishing village, nestled above a glassy cove. 'Just twenty miles long and eight miles wide. But we like it. And the Romeros haven't allowed it to become too commercialised.'

The Romeros. Eve wondered if there was any part of the island that didn't depend on the Romeros' approbation to survive. She doubted it. What was it Cassie had said? Jake's family owned the island? Yes, that was it. She wondered again if she wasn't being all kinds of a fool in coming here.

'I understand the school where you used to work has closed?' Isabel said suddenly, making Eve wonder what else might have been said about her.

'It closes in about a week's time,' she agreed, feeling a momentary twinge of homesickness for her grandmother and Watersmeet, and all the people she'd known there. 'Do—er—do you have many pupils at your school, Miss Rodrigues?'

'*My* school?' Isabel laughed. 'It's not my school, Miss Robertson. My mother's the academic, not me.'

'Oh.' Eve was embarrassed. 'I'm sorry. I didn't—'

'You thought because I'm called Rodrigues, I must be *the* Rodrigues,' Isabel said, with an amused sideways glance. 'No. My mother's the head teacher of San Felipe Primary. And, please, call me Isabel. Miss Rodrigues is so formal—Miss Robertson.'

'Eve,' said Eve at once. 'So you don't teach—um—Isabel?'

'Heavens, no.' Isabel grimaced. 'I work for Jake. At the boat yard. I handle all the bookings, the correspondence. I suppose you could say I'm his personal assistant.'

Eve nodded, unable to think of anything positive to say to that news. She should have known a man like Jake Romero would surround himself with beautiful people, beautiful women. Like her mother...

They were approaching the suburbs of what appeared to be a small town, and Isabel slowed accordingly. 'This is San Felipe,' she said, gesturing towards the rows of houses, the small shopping centre that developed as they approached the centre of town. 'This is where most people live, but the school is about half a mile beyond the town, nearer the tourist part of the island.'

'Are there hotels?' asked Eve, surprised to find the place so sophisticated.

'Small hotels,' agreed Isabel, swerving to avoid a bus that was lumbering towards them on the wrong side of the road. 'But the people who come here are mostly deep-sea fishermen, divers—people like that.'

'I see.'

Eve tugged her braid over one shoulder to cool her nape, and hoped it wasn't much further. Tiredness was catching up with her. Long journeys did that to her, and she hadn't really slept well since she'd accepted the job.

Beyond the outskirts of the small town, Isabel turned onto a narrow track that led down towards the sea. A coast road hugged the rim of dunes that were dotted here and there with wildflowers, and further on a clutch of white-roofed houses were clustered beside a wooden jetty. The bleached stumps of a groyne jutted out into the shallow waters, and on the beach below the village several fishing boats had been drawn up onto the sand.

'We're here,' said Isabel, waving at a handful of children who stopped playing to watch them go by. 'The school's just along here, and your house is just a little further on.'

'My house!' Eve was startled. 'I have a house?'

'Jake thought you'd prefer it,' Isabel said carelessly, but Eve sensed there was an edge of resentment in her voice now. 'The previous schoolteacher lodged with us. My Mom and me, that is.'

'I see.' Eve didn't know what to say. 'It sounds—wonderful. I've never had a home of my own before.'

'No?' Isabel sounded a little less disapproving as she glanced her way. 'Well, it's very small. Just a through living room and kitchen, with a bedroom and bathroom across a hallway. Typical San Felipe design. Simple and practical.'

'Just what I need,' said Eve, wondering if Jake hadn't been a little ambitious on her behalf. What did she really know about looking after herself? And how on earth was she supposed to get supplies?

An hour later most of her questions had been answered. Isabel had taken her first to meet her mother, the headmistress of the school. School being out for the day, Mrs Rodrigues was at home, and Eve soon realised that compared to what Isabel had described the Rodrigueses' home was considerably more spacious.

Isabel's mother, reassuringly, was not unlike Mrs Portman, and she was obviously eager to make her new employee feel at home. She suggested Eve should take a couple of days to acclimatise herself to the island, and invited her to have dinner with herself and Isabel the following evening.

'You'll find your fridge stocked, and drinking water in the taps,' she went on. 'We're lucky here on San Felipe. We have plenty of water, and it's perfectly safe to drink.'

Eve also discovered she had an open-topped buggy for her use, sitting to one side of her cottage. 'There are buses,' said Isabel, who had driven the few yards from her home with Eve's luggage, 'but they're not very reliable. Besides, you'll want to see something of the island while you're here.'

It was those last three words that occupied Eve's thoughts as she unpacked her belongings. What did they mean? Was it just Isabel's way of being friendly? Or was she implying that Eve wouldn't stay too long? And, if so, why? Did Jake have anything to do with it? To do with Isabel?

But that idea was not conducive to a relaxed first evening in her new home. And, after taking a deliciously cool shower to refresh herself, Eve checked the fridge.

She wasn't particularly hungry. Bearing in mind it was already late in the evening in Falconbridge, she just wanted something to tide her over until the morning. But she also knew that if she went to bed too early she'd be awake again before it was light.

She prepared herself an avocado salad from the makings she'd found in the fridge, and ate it at the Formica-topped kitchen table. Then she poured herself a glass of diet cola and carried it out onto the veranda at the back of the house. A pair of battered canvas chairs were set in the shade of a striped awning, and Eve sank into one, grateful for the comparative coolness of the night air.

It was almost completely dark now, and although she could still hear the sound of the ocean she could no longer see the water creaming into the cove just a few yards away. But in the morning the view would be waiting for her, she thought, hardly able to believe she was really here. She would have to phone her grandmother in the morning, too, but for tonight she was content just to let the peace and tranquillity of her surroundings drift over her.

She thought she might have fallen asleep for a few minutes, because the unusual sound of a car's engine gave her quite a start. She wasn't alarmed. Although there had been a little traffic past the cottage since her arrival, there were a few dwellings beyond her own.

But then she realised the car had stopped, and presently she heard the sound of boot heels on the flagged path that ran along the side of the house. She blinked. What time was it, for goodness sake? *Eleven!* She should have been in bed hours ago.

Her heart quickened instinctively. She had the feeling she knew exactly who her visitor was, but that didn't stop the panicky wave of excitement that swept over her at the thought of seeing him again. But she would have preferred not see him tonight—not now, when she was feeling so vulnerable. She wished she'd had the sense to turn the lights out before venturing onto the veranda. If there'd been no lights, he wouldn't have stopped. As it was, with the blinds undrawn, illuminating the area like a beacon, she had no choice but to admit to being awake.

Getting up from her chair, she moved to the veranda rail, deliberately putting herself in shadow. He might have the advantage of surprise, but she'd see his expression before he saw hers.

However, when Jake turned the corner, where a flight of shallow wooden steps led up to where she was standing, her heart almost stopped beating altogether. In a sleeveless cotton tee shirt, with baggy khaki shorts brushing his knees, he was just as disturbing as ever, and she realised that, whatever the circumstances, she had no advantage at all when it came to this man.

'Hi,' he said, placing one hand on the stair-rail. 'Can I come up?'

Eve made a careless movement with her shoulders. 'It's your house,' she said, which wasn't exactly an invitation, and, moving back to her chair, she sank down again onto her seat.

Jake took a deep breath and climbed the stairs, even though every nerve in his body was telling him he shouldn't do this. He hadn't intended to come here. When he'd left his house he'd only intended to drive past the cottage, just to assure himself that all was well. That was his excuse, anyway. But then he'd seen the light, and he hadn't been able to resist it. He hadn't realised how much he'd needed to see her again until he'd stopped the car.

'You're up late,' he said, pausing at the top of the steps and resting his back against the post. He wished there was more light, so that he could see her clearly, but what he could see tightened his stomach and quickened his pulse. 'I thought you'd be asleep by now.'

Eve glanced his way. 'Is that why you waited until now to come by? Because you thought I'd be asleep?'

'No.' Jake shoved his hands into the pockets of his shorts, so she wouldn't see the way they'd convulsed at her words. 'I was out for a drive and I saw the light.'

'Isn't it a little late to be out for a drive?' She was sardonic.

Jake shrugged. 'By your standards, maybe. Me—I don't sleep that well.'

Which was nothing but the truth. Since he'd got back from England he hadn't had above half a dozen decent nights' sleep.

Eve looked up at him now. He thought she looked a little concerned, but he couldn't honestly tell in the half-light that illuminated her face.

'Perhaps if you went to bed earlier?' she murmured, raising the glass in her hand to her lips. Then, seeing him watching her, 'I suppose I should offer you some refreshment, shouldn't I?'

Jake's conscience advised him to say no. He had no sense, being here, and he wasn't going to do himself any favours if he let her offer him a drink, if he went into the house.

But the temptation to see her properly overcame everything else. 'That would be nice,' he said, straightening away from the stair-post. 'Do you have a beer?'

Eve got up from her seat. 'Don't you know?' she threw over her shoulder as she opened the door. A huge moth tried to get in and she batted it away before adding tersely, 'Come and see.'

It was years since Jake had been inside one of these cottages, and he was immediately struck by how shabby they had become. He made a brief mental note to have a decorator check them out and update where necessary— which looked about everywhere—but his thoughts were summarily put on hold when he looked at Eve again.

She was wearing a short pink skirt that exposed her long legs, and he thought what a waste it had been to hide them with trousers. She had on a matching top, also different for her, with the kind of spaghetti straps he longed to undo. Was she wearing a bra? he wondered. He didn't think so. She hadn't been expecting visitors, after all. But that didn't stop the sudden rush of blood to his groin.

If Eve was aware of his intent regard, she ignored it, reaching into the fridge and extracting an icy-cold can of lager from the rack in the door. 'Will this do?'

'Thanks.'

Jake took the can from her, flipped the tab, and drank half its contents in one gulp. God, he'd needed that, he thought. He hadn't failed to notice how she'd avoided touching him when she handed him the beer. And, despite her latent hospitality, he was fairly sure she couldn't wait for him to leave.

'So,' he said, watching her as she crossed her arms over her midriff and turned to rest her back against the fridge door, 'you had a good journey?'

A strange look crossed her face at this question, and he wasn't really surprised when her response was equally oblique. 'Haven't you spoken to your spy?'

'My spy?' Jake did a double-take. 'I don't have a spy.'

'But you did send Miss Rodrigues to meet me, didn't you?' she queried, tucking her fingertips beneath her arms. The action caused her folded arms to press hard against her breasts, and Jake was momentarily diverted by an urgent desire to take their place.

Which he *so* mustn't do.

Forcing himself to meet her eyes, he said, 'I sent Isabel to meet you, yeah. I was pretty sure you wouldn't want to see my ugly mug the minute you got off the plane.'

'Oh, please. Only someone who didn't have an "ugly

mug'', as you put it, would say something like that!' she exclaimed, and he arched a mocking brow.

'Is that a compliment?'

'It was an observation,' she told him flatly. 'I'm tired, Jake. Why have you really come here?'

Because I couldn't keep away?

No, that wouldn't work. 'I thought I told you,' he began earnestly. 'I was—'

'—passing and you saw the light,' she finished cynically. 'Yes, I heard what you said.' She waited a beat. 'Do you expect me to thank you for offering me this job?'

Jake expelled a shocked breath. 'That was a low blow, even for you.'

'Why even for me?' Eve's lips pursed. 'Because I'm Cassie's daughter?' She took a steadying breath. 'I am nothing like my mother.'

'D'you think I don't know that?' Jake stifled an oath at the realisation they'd got off on the wrong foot again. 'After what I've learned about your mother, I wouldn't insult you by even implying you were.'

Eve's brows drew together. 'After what you've learned about my mother?' she echoed. 'What do you mean by that? What has she told you?'

'The truth?' he suggested drily. 'As your grandmother set the ball rolling, there wasn't much else she could do.'

Eve felt sick. 'So you know about—about the Fultons and—and Andy Johnson?'

'I know you've had a pretty tough time,' he said harshly, disliking the humiliated look she gave him. 'Eve, this isn't about the past, or about your mother. Offering you this job—I just wanted to help you, that's all.' He shook his head. 'There are no strings attached.'

Eve's smoky gaze slid over his for a moment, then dropped to the floor. For the first time he noticed she was barefoot, and for some reason that was as sexy as hell. But what she was saying sobered him, and forced him to meet her wary gaze. 'You—you went to see Cassie before you left London?'

Jake was taken aback. He wouldn't have thought her mother would have advertised that interview. 'Yes,' he said evenly. 'Yes, I did. Does it matter?'

'Why did you go to see her?'

'You know why.' He lifted a hand to massage the sudden ache he'd developed in the back of his neck. 'You can't drop a pebble into a still pool without expecting the ripples to spread.'

A tremor ran over her as he spoke. 'It was nothing to do with you.'

'Like hell it wasn't.' He was trying to keep his temper, but she could hear the anger underlying his harsh words. 'I wanted to know why she'd abandoned her daughter. Your grandmother had only given me the bare bones of the story. I wanted to hear it from her own lips.'

'Why? Why should it matter to you?'

'Just accept that it does, right?' he said shortly. He thrust the empty can onto the drainer and pushed his balled fist into his palm. 'Look, it was obviously a mistake to come here tonight—'

'You couldn't keep away from her, could you?'

'What?'

'Cassie. You slept with her again, didn't you?' She shivered suddenly, as if she was cold. 'When Ellie phoned to tell her I was taking this job, she asked her to warn me not trust you. I didn't understand what she meant then, but now I do.' She shook her head. 'Not that I needed the warning. You—'

She didn't get to finish what she was saying. He covered the space between them in one stride, grasping her shoulders and hauling her up so that only the tips of her toes touched the floor. Then his mouth was on hers, hard and bruising, plundering her lips with all the power and expertise of which she already knew he was capable.

And despite everything she melted.

Her breath escaped against his lips as they parted, and then his tongue was in her mouth and she was having difficulty hanging onto her sanity, let alone her balance.

'You knew I'd come, didn't you?' he muttered, his mouth hot and demanding, but sensually appealing. 'You can accuse me of that, yet you knew I'd come.' His hand slid into the coils of the braid that she'd loosened earlier, his thumb abrading the fine cords in her throat that were drawn as taut as violin strings. He swore again. 'I am so predictable.'

She was breathing too quickly, her heart thundering in her ears. She could feel herself getting dizzy, but it didn't matter because this was where she wanted to be and she couldn't pull away.

'You're not predictable at all,' she mumbled, but she doubted he could hear her. Besides, the heat of his body, the hard pressure of his shaft throbbing against her hip, had a hypnotic quality. She felt as if she was floating several inches above the ground.

His hands stroked the sensitive curve of her spine and she couldn't help arching against him, inviting God knew what. 'I couldn't keep away,' he said, almost savagely, cupping her bottom and urging her into even closer contact with his aroused body. 'I had to see you. Pathetic, huh? Particularly as you're prepared to believe the worst of me whatever I do.'

'No.' Eve's head was swimming and she was hardly aware of what she was saying. She didn't want to talk; she didn't even want to think. She just wanted him to go on kissing her and kissing her, drugging her with his mouth and his tongue until her brain joined her senses in a total meltdown. 'Jake, it doesn't matter—'

'It does to me.'

As suddenly as he'd taken hold of her, he uttered an oath and she was free. She stood swaying in front of him, trying to comprehend why he was looking at her with such contempt now when only moments before he had been seducing her with his lips and his hands, but her mind simply couldn't handle it.

'Jake—'

'I did not sleep with Cassandra,' he informed her harshly. 'And if you think I did then I'm just wasting my time.'

'I—I didn't say that—'

'Forget it.' Jake made for the door. 'I already have.'

CHAPTER TWELVE

JAKE was going over the navigation charts with one of his skippers in the cabin of his latest acquisition when he heard the sound of high-heeled footsteps on the deck above.

For a moment he entertained the crazy notion of how he'd feel if it was Eve invading his space. But he knew that wasn't going to happen. Although she was still on the island, working at the school and proving popular with staff and parents by all accounts, she was unlikely to want to see him.

In fact, he hadn't spoken to her since the night she'd arrived, almost five weeks ago. Granted, he'd been away for part of that time, attending boat shows in Japan and South America, but he was fairly sure she was doing her best to avoid him.

Which wasn't easy on an island as small as San Felipe. Jake had actually seen her several times, but always from a distance. He didn't want to admit it, but even after all that had happened she was seldom out of his thoughts, and seeing her, even from fifty yards away, was becoming as necessary to him as breathing.

That was why he'd prevailed upon the good-natured head teacher of the school to offer her the job in the first place. In actual fact there'd been no job as such, although according to Mrs Rodrigues Eve was proving a definite asset. Her arrival had enabled class sizes to be reduced, and, having worked in an English school, she was able to offer the most up-to-date methods of teaching.

'Jake! Are you there?'

His mother's voice called from above, and after bestowing an apologetic look in Dan Cassidy's direction, Jake moved to the foot of the stairs.

'Yeah, I'm here,' he said, and, realising she wouldn't be happy conducting a conversation from this distance, he gripped the rail and started up. 'Is everything okay?'

'Yes. Why wouldn't it be?' To his relief, she'd taken off her shoes in deference to the white-painted deck and was presently seated in the pilothouse, her legs raised to rest comfortably on the dark blue leather seats. 'So this is the new addition to the fleet?'

'It is.' Jake reached the open doorway, propped a shoulder against the frame and folded his arms. 'Do you like it?'

His mother shrugged her shoulders in a careless gesture. Despite being brought up in Massachusetts, where sailing was practically a way of life, she'd never been interested in boats. Her trim five-feet-two-inch frame was more at home on the golf course, or at the wheel of her Mercedes coupé, which was why Jake was surprised to see her here, apparently showing some interest in his job.

'It's very nice,' she said, and Jake pulled a wry face at the unenthusiastic description.

'Damned with faint praise,' he said drily. 'Okay. So that's not why you're here.'

'Well, no.' Lucy Romero swung her legs to the floor and smoothed the skirt of her cream silk suit over her knees. Then she smiled up at him. 'We haven't seen you for some time. I was wondering if you were all right, actually.'

Jake managed a forced laugh. 'You're kidding, right? I see Dad practically every day.'

'At the office or here,' she said dismissively. 'You haven't been over for dinner in weeks.'

Jake shrugged. 'I've been busy.'

'Doing what, exactly? Your father tells me you spend most of your evenings on your own. When was the last time you accepted an invitation to a party? How long is it since you've seen your brother and his wife? I'll tell you—months!'

'I didn't realise you were keeping tabs on my movements,' said Jake a little tersely, straightening from his lounging position and walking towards the bank of instruments at the front of the cabin. 'I'm not twenty-one any more, Mom.'

'What's that supposed to mean?'

'Think about it. The last time you got involved in my affairs I ended up married to Holly Bernstein.' He glanced at her over his shoulder. 'Enough said?'

'Holly was a lovely girl.'

'But not for me,' said Jake flatly. 'No matter how much you and her mother tried to keep us together. Holly was an airhead, Mom. I've got no time for women like that.'

'Haven't you?' His mother sounded snappish now. 'Well, perhaps not recently, no. But from what I hear they used to be the only women you did have time for.'

Jake sighed. 'Perhaps that's because they don't expect more than I'm prepared to give them?' He shook his head. 'Leave it, Mom. I'm happy the way I am.'

'Are you?' She looked doubtful. Then, her eyes dropping the length of his lean frame, she added, 'You've lost weight.'

Jake groaned. 'Mom!'

'Well, all your father and I want is for you to be happy.'

'Then leave me alone.'

'I can't do that.' She caught her lower lip between her

teeth. 'Come for dinner tomorrow evening. Please, Jake. I'll get Rosa to make your favourite meringue dessert.'

He turned to rest against the chart desk. 'You don't give up, do you?'

'Would you want me to?'

Jake gave her a wry smile. 'I guess not.'

'So you'll come?'

'Do I have a choice?'

'Oh, good.' His mother got up from the banquette and came to give him a hug. 'Shall we say—seven o'clock?'

Jake frowned. 'That sounds awfully formal. This isn't a dinner party, is it?'

'Just one or two friends,' said Lucy innocently. 'Now, you can't back out, Jake. You've said you'll come and I'm holding you to it.'

Eve heaved a deep breath and surveyed her appearance in the bathroom mirror without enthusiasm. The little black dress that her grandmother had bought her, which had looked so good back in England, had looked totally out of place here. Which was why she'd been obliged to splash out on an alternative. But now that she had no choice except to wear what she'd bought, she was definitely having misgivings. What did one wear to a dinner party in San Felipe? Particularly one where Jake Romero might be present?

She shivered. She'd gone with the simple ivory silk jersey that the salesgirl in town had assured her was perfect for the occasion, but now she wasn't so sure. It seemed too low cut, it showed too much of her arms, of her body, and it was definitely too short. The only thing she liked was the gold chain-link belt that circled her hips. It might divert attention from the rounded curve of her bottom, but she doubted it. She should have stuck with the long-sleeved grey sheath she'd chosen to begin with.

She sighed. She wasn't sure about her hairstyle either. Despite Isabel's assurances that long hair simply wasn't practical in this climate, having it cut at all had been a stretch. It was still long enough to put in a ponytail for school, but tonight she'd left it loose, and it was odd having its heavy weight swinging against her cheeks.

Still, Isabel had been enthusiastic, and as she and Mrs Rodrigues' daughter had become friends in recent weeks Eve hadn't liked to disappoint her by voicing her doubts. And there was no question that it was cooler this way. She just wished she'd never been offered an invitation to the Romeros' villa in the first place.

It wasn't as if Jake had anything to do with it. She hadn't laid eyes on him since the evening she'd arrived on the island, and from gossip she'd heard around school he'd been keeping a very low profile in recent weeks.

She knew he'd been away for part of the time. She'd heard that from one of the workmen who'd arrived to paint and decorate the cottage. On his orders, apparently. Evidently he hadn't liked it the way it was.

No, the reason she was attending this dinner party was because of Mrs Rodrigues. The head teacher and her daughter had both been invited, but Mrs Rodrigues had developed a severe cold the day before, and she had prevailed upon Eve to accompany Isabel in her place.

'I've spoken to Lucy Romero—that's Jake's mother, you know—and she's quite happy for you to join them,' Mrs Rodrigues had explained comfortably. 'Besides, you'll enjoy it far more than I would.'

Eve had wanted to say that she wouldn't enjoy it at all, but she couldn't do that. It simply wouldn't be true. She told herself it was because she didn't want to disappoint

Mrs Rodrigues or Isabel, but if she was totally honest with herself she'd admit that she was aching to see Jake again. Which was ridiculous, of course, but it did account for all the soul-searching she was suffering now.

A perfunctory knock, followed by Isabel calling her name, heralded her friend's arrival. Eve cast one last look at herself before going out to meet her, determined to find some excuse not to go if Isabel showed any doubts about her appearance.

But in fact Isabel looked stunned when she saw her. Her dark eyes widened with amazement as she took in Eve's appearance, and her, 'Oh—you look nice,' was said in the most half-hearted of tones.

Eve blew out a breath. 'Do you think so?' she asked anxiously, suddenly realising that, despite what the other girl had said, Isabel's hair was fairly long. She usually wore it coiled in a chignon at her nape, so Eve hadn't realised how long it actually was. But this evening it was loose, an ebony cape over one shoulder, threaded with silver beads to match her long gown.

'Well, you certainly look different,' Isabel declared now, and Eve wondered if she was only imagining the tartness in her voice. 'You're a dark horse, Eve. I'd never have recognised you. Compared to the way you dress for school...'

'It's not suitable?' Despite a sudden wariness about Isabel's attitude, Eve didn't have the confidence to trust her own judgement.

'I didn't say that.' There was no mistaking the terseness now. Isabel glanced at the jewelled watch on her wrist and clicked her tongue. 'In any case, we've got to go. I don't want to be late.'

It wasn't the most auspicious way to start the evening, and Eve fretted about what she was doing all the way to the Romero house. Fortunately Isabel had agreed to drive them in her sports car—with the hood up this time, to protect them from the breeze—which meant she had to concentrate on the road instead of her companion. Which suited Eve very well.

Although Eve had never been to Jake's parents' house, of course, she knew roughly where it was. It occupied a beautiful peninsula of land a couple of miles south of San Felipe. It was set back from the road, behind a hedge of flowering hibiscus, and according to one of the other teachers it was quite a showplace.

The marina, where the Romeros' charter company had its headquarters, was in town, and Eve had wandered along the quay there, admiring the many beautiful yachts at their moorings. She'd worn dark glasses, of course, just in case she'd seen Jake, but she'd never glimpsed anyone who remotely resembled him.

'Here we are.'

Isabel was braking hard now, throwing Eve forward as they swept between open wrought-iron gates. A short drive along an avenue of palm trees strung with lights brought them to a forecourt, with an illuminated fountain. One or two cars were already parked to one side of the forecourt, in front of a row of garages, and Isabel parked beside them and pulled her keys out of the ignition.

In other circumstances Eve might have been intimidated, but she was so busy admiring the sprawling two-storey villa that she forgot to be alarmed. A wraparound balcony on the first floor would give a wonderful view of the sea that lapped at both sides of the peninsula, she thought, and the warm sandstone walls were liberally covered with bougainvillaea and other climbing tropical plants.

'Impressive, isn't it?' Although Isabel had barely spoken on the journey, she now seemed to remember her manners. 'Jake's grandfather built this place just after the first World War.'

'It's beautiful,' said Eve, getting out of the car and looking about her. Apprehension was gripping her, however. 'Um—I suppose you know the Romeros very well?'

'I've known them all my life,' said Isabel, which wasn't quite an answer. But then a white-jacketed steward appeared and she grasped Eve's arm. 'Come along. We're expected.'

As they climbed shallow stone steps to the entry, Eve wondered if that was true. Isabel was expected, certainly, but who had Mrs Rodrigues said she was sending in her place?

Whatever, she had no time to worry about that now. Even as her eyes were drawn to a lamplit terrace, where a handful of scarlet-cushioned lounge chairs were set amongst a forest of greenery, a dainty blonde-haired woman came out of the double doors to greet them.

'Isabel!' she exclaimed, reaching for the young woman's hands and drawing her in for an air-kiss beside each cheek. 'How lovely to see you again. What a pity your mother couldn't join us, too. I hope she'll feel better soon.'

'I'm sure she will, Mrs Romero.' Isabel was warmly affable now, no trace of her earlier irritation in her beaming face. 'Oh, and let me introduce you to one of my mother's teachers, Eve Robertson. She came out from England just a few weeks ago.'

'Ah, yes. I believe I've heard of Miss Robertson.' Eve was taken aback when Jake's mother took her hand and gazed up at her with shrewd, assessing eyes. 'I think my son was instrumental in your being offered the post, Miss

Robertson.' She paused. 'Am I right in thinking you got to know one another while he was in London?'

'I—that's right.' Eve decided there was no point in complicating matters by describing how they'd really met. 'It was kind of you to invite me, Mrs Romero.' She moistened her dry lips. 'You have a beautiful home.'

'Thank you. We like it.' Jake mother seemed genuinely pleased with the compliment. 'Well, come and meet the rest of the family. Jake's not here yet, but I'm expecting him to join us very shortly.'

Grateful for small mercies, Eve followed Isabel and their hostess into a large reception hall that was lit by a huge crystal chandelier. Perhaps a dozen other people were standing about in groups, enjoying the Romeros' hospitality. There was music and laughter, and a buzz of small talk that died down significantly when Jake's mother appeared with the two young women.

A grey-haired man, who had to be Jake's father, joined them, and it was he who introduced Eve to Jake's brother, Michael, and his wife, Julie. Julie was heavily pregnant, but she still looked elegant in a form-fitting satin sheath that skimmed her knees. To Eve's relief, she saw most of the women were wearing short dresses, the men less formal in casual shirts and trousers.

Julie seemed to take an instant liking to Eve, and when her father-in-law would have moved on, she said, 'I suppose you find island life a little confining, Miss Robertson?' She tucked a strand of dark red hair behind her ear as she spoke. 'I know I did when I first came here.'

'It's—different,' began Eve, but before she could continue Isabel intervened.

'That's because you're not an islander,' she said dispassionately. 'And if you don't like it you can always go back to England.'

Was that a suggestion or a warning? Eve wondered, as Julie rolled her eyes behind the other woman's back. 'We all know you love San Felipe, Isabel,' she remarked, taking a sip of the mineral water she was drinking. 'But, you know, you're the one who should consider spreading her wings.'

Isabel's lips tightened, but Jake's brother chose to lighten the mood. 'Do you find teaching a rewarding occupation, Miss Robertson?' he enquired easily. 'I can't imagine having the patience to handle one infant, let alone a handful.'

'You'd better get used to it,' declared his wife at once, and everyone laughed.

'Please, call me Eve.' Eve could feel herself relaxing. Michael was like his brother in so many ways, but without the sexual edge.

And then, as Jake's father was handing her the cocktail she'd chosen, she was suddenly aware that someone else had entered the room. She had no reason for the feeling. It wasn't as if someone had announced his arrival. But long before she heard Michael greeting his brother she knew that Jake was there.

She couldn't resist looking over her shoulder at him. It seemed a lifetime since she'd seen him, and knowing he was just across the room brought back all the feelings she'd tried to convince herself she could control.

She knew at once that she'd been wasting her time. She wasn't going to get Jake Romero out of her system by ignoring him, or by pretending that what had been between them meant nothing to her. She was very much afraid it had gone beyond a mere attraction; she was falling in love with him. Even the thought of sharing him with another woman was more bearable than never seeing him, never touching him again.

She caught her breath when their eyes met, and she saw the shock of recognition in his gaze. Obviously his mother hadn't shared her guest list with him, and she wondered if he resented the fact that she was here, in his parents' home.

She closed her eyes for a moment, taking a deep breath, praying for her palpitating heart to subside. It felt as if a whole river of perspiration was flowing down between her breasts, and her dress was clinging wetly to her spine.

Which was ridiculous, considering the room was air-conditioned, but her body seemed to be reacting independently of her brain. Even behind her lids she could see him, so lean and dark and attractive. And so incredibly male.

She was jolted out of her introspection by hard fingers closing about her upper arm. Opening her eyes, she was hardly surprised to find he'd come to stand beside her, or that his eyes were cool and guarded as they thoroughly appraised her appearance.

'I suppose this is where I'm supposed to say, What are you doing here?' he said roughly. 'Believe it or not, I didn't know you'd been invited. If I had I'd have made some excuse and stayed away.'

Eve wondered how she was supposed to answer that. It would be easy enough to counter his claim with a similar one of her own. But she couldn't do it. 'I didn't know if you'd be here either,' she ventured in a low voice, aware that their conversation was being monitored by other members of the party. 'I—I actually hoped you might be. Do you mind?'

Jake's fingers dug into her arm for a moment, and when she ventured a look at his face she saw his eyes were glittering with anger. Taking her glass from her unresisting fingers, he dumped it on a table. Then, after offering an apologetic word to those around them, he hustled Eve towards the sliding glass doors that led outside.

She didn't know what he intended to do. Perhaps this was his way of forcibly ejecting her, she thought, wondering what his parents must be thinking of his behaviour. Certainly there was aggression in the way he slammed open the door and pushed her unceremoniously out onto the patio at the back of the house. Then, with the door closed securely behind them, he virtually frogmarched her towards an unlit portion of the garden.

Eve was wearing high heels, and her ankles were aching when he finally called a halt. With a trellis of night-flowering honeysuckle between them and any prying eyes that might be watching them from the salon, and only the moon for illumination, he swung her round to face him and said savagely, 'Do you enjoy making a fool of me?'

CHAPTER THIRTEEN

'I WASN'T. I didn't.' Eve blinked. His face was in shadow, but she could feel the anger emanating from him. 'I don't know what you're talking about.'

'Like hell you don't. The last time we were together—'

'You walked out on me,' she broke in defensively, and she heard his snort of frustration. 'Well, you did.'

'And you know why,' Jake retorted, and when he lifted his hand to rake back his hair, which had grown longer over the past few weeks, she saw the faint tremor that shook his arm. 'You accused me of sleeping with your mother. Again.' He swore. 'I've never slept with your mother, *ever*. What do you take me for?'

Eve quivered now. 'That—that's what she said.'

'And since when do you believe anything that woman tells you?' he demanded, resisting the urge to shake her.

'You went away,' Eve said helplessly. 'Wh—what was I supposed to think?'

Jake grabbed her arm, as if he needed to hold onto her for support. Then he said hoarsely, 'You wanted me to go away. You told me there could never be anything between us because—because of your mother.'

'I know.' She took a trembling breath. 'But—you didn't argue, did you?'

'Oh, right.' Jake's fingers dug into her wrist. 'You just deliver the biggest bombshell of my life and I'm not supposed to show any reaction? Get real, Eve. I was mad. Mad as hell. With Cassandra, with you, but most especially with myself.'

'Because—because you thought I'd made a fool of you?'

'Do you blame me?' His thumb caressed the fine network of veins he'd found on the inner side of her arm, the roughness in his voice scraping across her nerves like raw silk. 'You should have told me who you were,' he said harshly. 'How you came to be living with your grandmother. That night in the library, for example. Then I might have understood why you'd gone to pieces because another man had forced his attentions on you.'

'It was only a kiss,' said Eve, with a shudder.

'But it meant more than that to you?'

'Yes.' Eve glanced up at him. And then, because she wanted him to understand, she went on, 'It reminded me of all the nights I'd spent sleeping in the bathroom when I lived with the Fultons.' Her lips twisted. 'It was the only room in the house that had a lock on the door.'

Jake groaned. 'Didn't you tell anyone?'

'Yes, I told Emily. This was his wife. But she didn't believe me.' She shrugged. 'Or perhaps she didn't want to know. Anyway, that's why I ran away.'

Jake swore. 'I'm so sorry, baby.' He bent his head and rested his forehead against hers. 'God, Cassandra has a lot to answer for.'

Eve's knees felt weak. 'To—to be fair, she knew nothing about it,' she ventured huskily, lifting one hand to cup his cheek, and he turned his mouth against her palm.

'Do you think that excuses her?' he exclaimed unsteadily. 'No wonder you wanted nothing to do with me.'

'That's not true.' Eve couldn't let him think that. 'You—you confused me. Until then I'd never been attracted to any man. I firmly believed I never would be. I thought I was quite happy, living with Ellie and doing my job. I—I didn't want anything else.'

'And?'

'And so when you came along I resented you. Resented how you made me feel.'

Jake's eyes darkened. 'How did I make you feel?'

'You know,' she protested.

'Perhaps I do.' He paused. 'Perhaps I just want to hear it from your lips.'

Eve shook her head. 'I just knew it was wrong, that's all. I thought you were with Cassie and I had no right feeling anything where you were concerned.'

'But you did?'

'You know I did,' she said shyly. 'Even that night in the library, I— Well, I knew then that you weren't like anyone else I'd ever known.'

Jake covered her hand with one of his. 'I wish you'd told me.'

'How could I?'

'Oh, baby.' He allowed a long sigh to escape him. 'Cassandra and I were never an item. I think that was why she invited me to Watersmeet.'

'So why did you come?'

'Believe it or not, I was asking myself that question from the moment we left London.' His tongue brushed her palm for a moment, but then he controlled himself again and continued, 'I've got no excuse. I was bored, I guess, and I thought it might be interesting to see another part of the country. It wasn't until I met you that I realised that fate must have had a hand in it.'

Eve gazed up at him. 'You don't really mean that?'

'Don't I?' He tucked a strand of silky hair behind her ear. 'I thought I did. If you're talking about what happened after I kissed you in the stables, then I have to admit I don't take rejection very well.'

Eve could hardly breathe. 'You know why I said what I did.'

'I know.' Jake regarded her intently. 'So what's changed?'

'Everything. Nothing.' Eve lifted her shoulders in a gesture of defeat. 'Why are we having this conversation? You offered me a job. Was it, as you said, just because you wanted to help me? Or—or something else?'

Jake's hands slid along her forearms to her elbows. 'What else could it be?' he asked slyly, and her heart did a somersault in her chest.

'I don't know.' She'd go so far, but no further. 'Are you still angry with me? Is that what you're saying? Because if you are—'

But Jake couldn't let her continue. 'I was teasing,' he said roughly, drawing her up on her toes and bending his head to bestow a long, lingering kiss on her soft mouth. 'For pity's sake, Eve, you surely knew how I felt the night you arrived, when I came to the cottage.' His lips brushed her ear. 'God knows, I couldn't keep away.'

Eve trembled. 'You mean that, don't you?'

'I've never meant anything more in my life.'

'Oh, Jake!' She wound her arms around his neck and gazed into his eyes disbelievingly. 'I'm so afraid this is all a dream, and any minute I'm going to open my eyes and wake up.'

'I've had dreams like that, too,' said Jake fervently. 'Particularly when I thought you were going to let Cassandra ruin the rest of your life.'

Eve caught her breath. 'Did you think I would?'

Jake's eyes darkened. 'What was I supposed to think?'

She sighed. 'I suppose. Oh, Jake, weeks ago I realised I didn't care any more. About you and her, I mean. I just didn't know how I was going to tell you. Or—or if you'd care.'

'I care,' he said roughly, but before he could do more than cradle her head in his hands, and study her expectant face, they heard someone calling his name.

'Jake! Jake! Where are you? We're waiting to have dinner.'

'My mother,' said Jake drily, although he could see that Eve had already recognised her voice. He hesitated a moment. 'Are you very hungry?'

Eve gave a soft laugh. 'I'm not hungry at all.'

'I am,' Jake told her fiercely. 'But not for food.' He bent and gave her a swift kiss. 'Wait here.'

He was back a couple of minutes later, and Eve gave him an anxious look. 'Is she very angry?'

'My mother?' Jake laughed. 'Hell, no. Why should she be? She organised this dinner party to try and take me out of myself. She'll be delighted she's succeeded.'

'Oh, but—' Eve faltered. 'She doesn't know me.'

'She will soon.' Jake took her hand, leading the way through tall waving grasses to where low dunes edged a moonlit beach. 'I think Isabel was her original objective, but if she'd asked me I'd have told her she was wasting her time.' He glanced down. 'You might want to take off your shoes. The sand is damp.'

Eve did as he suggested, looking about her in wonder. 'It's so beautiful,' she said, as he took her shoes from her and dangled them from his free hand by their straps. Then, as he helped her down onto the beach, 'Are we going for a walk?'

'Initially,' he said enigmatically, starting along she shore. 'And before that agile mind of yours starts wondering about my association with Isabel, I should tell you that we've never been more than friends.'

Eve glanced up at him. 'I believe you.'

'You'd better.' He raised her hand to his lips and pressed a moist kiss to her palm. 'The truth is, my mother's known something was wrong ever since I got back from England. You won't have noticed, in my haste to get you alone, but I've lost weight, I don't sleep, and God knows I didn't know what the hell I was going to do next.'

Eve wrapped herself around his arm as they walked. 'You could have told me.'

'Yeah. Well, believe it or not, I was considering doing just that. Then I walked into the house tonight and there you were.' He pressed her close to his side. 'Can you wonder I reacted as I did?'

Eve leant her head on his shoulder. 'So what did your mother say when you spoke to her just now? Is she expecting us back?'

'Not any time soon,' said Jake drily. He paused, then said huskily, 'She just said, "Is she the one?" And I said yes.'

Eve could hardly breathe. She was filled with an excitement that was so intense she was amazed she could keep putting one foot in front of the other. She wanted to stop right then, and ask him to say what he'd said all over again. But although he looked down at her for a moment, before stealing another heartstopping kiss, he didn't slow his pace.

With dazed eyes, she forced herself to look where they were going. The shore was totally deserted, a pearl-white stretch of coral sand that gleamed in the moonlight. There were boulders here and there, rockpools that in daylight would reveal the tiny starfish and sand crabs that made the beach their home. And, although Jake's arm was reassuringly warm against her breasts, and his hip brushed hers as they walked, Eve still had the feeling that this was some incredible fantasy conjured up by her vivid imagination.

Then, when it looked as if they could go no further without scaling the cliffs that guarded the other end of the cove, Jake pointed to a villa that was set back behind the dunes. Low and sprawling, its creamy walls blended into its surroundings, and only the light spilling out from its windows advertised its existence.

'Come on,' he said. 'I want to show you where I live.'

Eve's lips parted. 'This is your house?'

'Mmm.' Jake slipped his arm around her. 'Come and see.'

Fifteen minutes later they were installed in Jake's living room. A long, open—plan area, with a huge stone fireplace he promised her he did use from time to time, it was modern without being ultra-trendy. The floors were polished teak, the trio of sofas were a blend of suede and leather, and the low table in front of the fireplace rested on a thick Chinese rug.

'It's beautiful,' said Eve, unable to think of any other adjective to use. 'Do you live here alone?'

'Apart from Luigi, yeah.' He had introduced her to his elderly Italian houseman when they arrived. 'Why? Did you think I kept a mess of women here for my own amusement?'

Eve, who was kneeling on an ivory leather sofa, watching him as he moved somewhat restlessly about the room, heaved a sigh. 'No,' she admitted honestly. 'But you did say you'd been married before.'

'Oh, yeah. For about six months.' Jake grimaced. 'And, for your information, we didn't live here. I had a condominium in San Felipe in those days.'

'I'm glad.' Eve bit her lip. 'Are you going to come and sit down?'

Jake glanced at the small bar set into the wall. 'Wouldn't you like a drink?'

'Would you?'

'No, but as I deprived you of the one my father made for you...'

'I don't want a drink.' Eve took a deep breath. 'I just want you to kiss me.'

Jake pulled a wry face. 'That's what I want, too.'

'So?'

'So that's not all I want,' he said, moving to the back of the sofa and looking down at her with dark intense eyes. 'And I don't know if I've got the will-power—or the strength—to limit myself to just kissing you.'

'Did I say I wanted you to?'

'Eve—' His hands covered hers where they rested on the soft leather, and she shivered a little in anticipation. 'We have to talk.'

'We'll talk later,' she promised him, capturing his hands in hers and drawing him around to the front of the sofa. Then she patted the seat beside her. 'Sit down.'

Jake did so, his weight depressing the cushions beside her so that even if she hadn't planned it that way she slid towards him. She grabbed him, to save herself, her hand slipping intimately over his thigh, and with a muffled oath he turned towards her, covering her startled lips with his.

His tongue invaded her mouth, hot and demanding, reminding her of his taste and his scent. She desperately wanted this, wanted to prove to him that she wasn't afraid of anything when she was with him, that he and he alone could erase all the pain and heartache of the past.

When he lifted his head and looked down at her she was devastated by his intensity. His lean face was taut with emotion, with feelings he was trying desperately hard to control. When he bent to her again there was a dangerous hunger in his invasion, a mind-numbing ardour that enveloped her in its thrall.

'You have no idea how much I've wanted to do this,' he groaned, tipping the straps of her dress aside and laving her shoulder with his tongue. 'I just don't want to hurt you.'

'You're not hurting me,' she protested, parting the neckline of his shirt and pressing her face against his hot skin. There was a film of moisture on his chest and she allowed herself to taste it, loving the way his flesh tensed at the intimate brush of her tongue. 'I couldn't stand it if you changed your mind now.'

'Dear God,' Jake muttered, as her dress slipped away to reveal the skimpy bra she was wearing beneath it. Two half-cups of cream lace barely contained the rounded breasts that were spilling out from them, dusky nipples hinting at the exotic cast of her colouring. 'I couldn't stand it either.'

She was all ebony and ivory, he thought, her skin pale, her hair so thick and dark against her cheeks. When he bent his head, to capture her mouth again, her hair swung against him and he felt its silken strands caress his face.

'Jake…'

His name was a heady sound on her lips. Hearing her use it in that seductive way was like drowning in sensation. His body stiffened automatically, and he thought she had no idea what she was doing to him. The swollen muscle between his legs was becoming a constant ache.

He found the fastener that secured the flimsy bra and dealt with it. Then, urging her back against the cushions, he positioned himself beside her. He didn't lie over her, although he wanted to. There was no way he could hide his arousal if he gave in to temptation.

Even so, he couldn't prevent himself from caressing her breasts, from lowering his head and taking one sensitive nipple into his mouth. She moaned softly, her pulse palpitating beneath his fingers, her hands reaching for him in mute acceptance of her own needs.

Her hands probed inside his collar, twining in the hair that grew longer at the nape of his neck. She was eager, too, he realised, wondering how long it was since she'd allowed any man to touch her. The boy she'd run away with—Andy Johnson?—had he been intimate with her? Jake thought he could gladly kill any man who'd touched her against her will.

She moved against him and he was sure she must feel his taut maleness against her hip. Her response, her willingness, was making him want to move faster than he'd intended, and when her legs parted he couldn't prevent his thigh from pushing urgently between hers.

'Ah, Eve,' he groaned, one hand sliding down to cup her bottom, moving beneath the short hem of her dress to find the soft skin at the top of her legs. She arched against his hand, and that almost drove him crazy. He so much wanted to be inside her, to feel her taut muscles urging him on.

Eve's head was spinning. There was increasing moisture between her legs, which she was sure he must have felt when he touched her there. She almost stopped breathing altogether when his fingers slid partway into her.

Acting purely on impulse, she trailed her hand down his chest to the waistband of his trousers. His shirt was half open anyway, and she completed the task. The buckle on his belt presented the next obstacle, but when she would have loosened it his hand stopped her

'Wait.' Jake's voice was hoarse, and she realised he was no more immune to her explorations than she was to his. 'I don't think you know what you're doing to me. I'm not made of stone, you know.'

'Nor am I,' she murmured, kissing his chest, loving the feel of his springing hair against her face. 'I want you, Jake. I want to make love with you. I don't want to be an oddball any more.'

'An oddball?' Jake gazed down at her with puzzled eyes. 'You're not an oddball.'

'Yes, I am.' Eve took a deep breath and continued, 'I've never let any man get close to me before.'

Jake shook his head. Cassandra really did have a lot to answer for, he thought again. 'Come,' he said softly, once again stopping her when she would have opened his zip to stroke his throbbing erection. 'I want to show you my bedroom. Besides, we don't want to risk being interrupted by Luigi asking if we want more ice.'

'Ice?' Eve felt a sob of laughter rising in her throat as Jake lifted her up into his arms and strode purposefully across the room.

'Not such a bad idea, in the circumstances,' agreed Jake huskily. 'Maybe some ice is exactly what we need.'

A flight of open-tread stairs gave access to the upper floor of the villa. Double doors stood wide into a huge master bedroom, with long oriel windows giving a magnificent view of the bay.

Jake laid Eve on the wide damask-covered bed. Only one lamp was burning, but beyond the windows the moon could be seen throwing a silver pathway over the sea. Its pale light added to the magical beauty of their surroundings, and when Jake lay down beside her she turned eagerly towards him.

Jake was gentle with her now, even though she sensed the urgency underlying his touch. Her dress had pooled about her waist, and she thought her bra must be somewhere between the bed and the sofa downstairs. But such insignificant considerations went out of her head when he bent to nibble at the creamy fullness of her breasts.

She wasn't able to stop herself from trembling, and he lifted his head again, to give her a searching look. 'Don't be alarmed,' he said. 'I like it that you're not so sophisticated. And that you don't honestly realise how sexy you are.'

Eve sucked in her breath. 'No one's ever called me that before.'

'Then they must have been blind,' said Jake thickly, feeling an increasing sense of euphoria at the knowledge that in many ways he was going to be first with her. In every way that mattered at least.

It was a simple matter to slide her dress down her hips, and, releasing one plump nipple, he allowed his tongue to trail a sensuous path from her breast to her navel. She quivered again, as he used his teeth to pull her lacy scrap of underwear away, and fairly bucked against him when he replaced his probing fingers with his tongue.

'You can't— You mustn't—' she began, but as he caressed her he saw the way her eyes grew dark with desire, and her breathing quickened in concert with her body's response.

She climaxed moments later, and he stifled her cry of wonder beneath the hungry pressure of his mouth. It pleased him enormously that she was so responsive, and this time when she reached for his buckle he didn't attempt to stop her.

Even so, it took all his self-control not to lose it completely when she took his thick shaft into her hands. But he wanted to be inside her when he found his own release, and, although she protested, he drew away to tear off his shirt and push his trousers down his legs.

Then he was beside her again, satisfying her impatience and his own by positioning himself above her. Eve knew a moment's panic when she saw how big he really was, but her legs parted willingly when he straddled her.

'Did I tell you that you're beautiful?' he breathed, and she felt the heat of his erection nudging her wet core.

He entered her in one almost smooth thrust, only briefly balked by the unmistakable barrier he encountered. Eve, who hadn't been prepared for the pain after the gentleness of his mouth, tried to stifle her moan of anguish against his throat, but it escaped anyway. She hadn't realised how much her body would rebel at this unfamiliar invasion; hadn't anticipated that it would hurt so much.

Nevertheless, when he withdrew again she was no less distressed. 'No,' she protested, but Jake was staring down at her in stunned disbelief.

'You were a virgin,' he said in a strangled voice. 'My God, why didn't you tell me?'

CHAPTER FOURTEEN

'I told you I was an oddball,' Eve whispered, trying to make light of it, but Jake wouldn't let her go on.

'You're not an oddball,' he exclaimed harshly, but once again Eve intervened.

'What would you call a twenty-five-year-old virgin?' she asked mockingly, but he laid a hard palm across her lips.

'Innocent,' he said tersely. 'God, I'm such an idiot. I thought—after what you'd been through—'

'Because of Graham Fulton?' Eve's lips twisted. 'I told you. I spent all my nights in the bathroom.' She pushed her lips against his palm for a moment, before drawing his hand away. 'And Andy Johnson knew how I felt, and he looked out for me.' She smiled. 'Until I met you, I couldn't bear a man to touch me, you see,' she confessed huskily. 'Ever since—ever since that man came to my room, I've always kept the opposite sex at arm's length.'

Jake groaned. 'Oh, baby, I've been such a fool.'

'It doesn't matter,' she protested, bringing his hand to her face and pressing it against her cheek. 'Not to me.' She waited a beat and then asked tremulously, 'You do still want me?'

Jake groaned again. 'Of course I want you. Now more than ever. But—'

'No buts,' said Eve firmly, levering herself up on her elbows and drawing his hands to her breasts. 'I've wanted you for so long. I couldn't bear it if you didn't feel the same.'

'Dear God!' Jake couldn't prevent himself from crushing her against the soft pillows of his bed. 'I think I've been waiting for you all my life,' he added shakily. His mouth possessed hers with the utmost tenderness. 'I just don't want to hurt you again.'

'You won't,' said Eve, not knowing how she knew this, but she did. 'Please.' Her fingers stroked his swollen erection. 'You can't stop now.'

Which was nothing less than the truth, thought Jake ruefully. But he wanted her to share his delight in their joining, and, although he still blamed himself for acting so recklessly, he ached to be inside her again.

Gently, he spread her legs and eased into her, using his lips and his tongue to relieve any anxiety she might feel. But, amazingly, she received him easily, her body slick and damp from her exertions.

And Jake was blown away again by her sweetness. She was everything he'd ever wanted in a woman, and the muscles in his gut tightened when they felt her willing response.

For Eve, it was equally as moving. Now that she knew what to expect, she welcomed his heat and the fullness his body created. But she was still unprepared for the feelings that surfaced when he withdrew partway before pushing into her again. They were like the feelings she'd had before, only deeper, stronger, causing a wave of expectation to sweep through her abdomen and up her spine until it felt as if she was tingling all over.

Almost instinctively, it seemed, she lifted her legs and wound them about his hips, holding him inside her. Jake took a steadying breath, trying to control the urge to quicken his pace, but it wasn't easy when he could feel the rippling wave of her orgasm tightening her muscles around him.

His body throbbed with the need for his own release, but once again he realised he was in danger of making another stupid mistake. The condom he should be using was still lying in the drawer of the table beside his bed. In his eagerness to make love with Eve he'd forgotten all about it, and he still had the sense to know that she wouldn't have done anything to protect herself.

Dammit, he thought, he couldn't do this to her. But when he attempted to withdraw she only tightened her long legs about him.

'Don't,' she whispered huskily, her breathing hot and unsteady against his throat, and Jake groaned.

'You don't understand—' he choked, but she only covered his mouth with hers.

'I do,' she breathed against his lips, and although he knew what he ought to do, the temptation to let her have her way was irresistible.

Besides, she was making frantic little sounds now that were totally driving him crazy. He was drenched with her scent, with her essence, and, giving in to a force that was stronger than he was, Jake spilled himself inside her.

His orgasm seemed to go and on, and when the shuddering pleasure had ceased he felt absolutely drained. But absolutely replete, too, which was something he'd never experienced before.

He realised suddenly that he was slumped on top of Eve, but when he would have rolled away she stopped him again. 'I've got to be crushing the breath out of you,' he protested, but she only wound her arms around his neck and gazed up at him with wide, adoring eyes.

'I don't care,' she said huskily. 'And before you say anything I don't care if I'm pregnant either.'

'Eve—'

'No, I mean it, Jake. And I don't want you to think it's

your responsibility. You're an honourable man, I know that, but this was my decision—'

'Stop! Stop right there!' Jake silenced her with a hard kiss, and before she could start again he exclaimed, 'For God's sake, I love you! I think I've loved you since the first moment I saw you. And if you think I'm going to let you go now, without a fight, you're very much mistaken.'

Eve's lips had parted for his kiss, but now, when he lifted his head, she found she needed to suck some much-needed air into her lungs. 'I—I don't know what to say.'

'Well, you could say you liked me just a little bit, too,' said Jake, trying to make light of his passionate declaration. Taking her arms from around his neck, he rolled onto his back beside her, staring up at the shadows that hid the ceiling. 'Unless I've jumped the gun again—'

'No!' Eve scrambled up now, to look down at him with anxious eyes. 'It's not that.' She made a helpless gesture. 'I just—well, it's like you said: you've taken my breath away.'

Jake lifted his hand to touch her cheek. 'But you knew I cared about you.'

Eve shook her head. 'My grandmother *cares* about me,' she said fiercely. 'You—you said you loved me.'

'I do.'

'But how can you?'

'How can I not?' he retorted, a little thickly. 'You're everything I've ever wanted, all rolled up in one delectable package.'

She quivered. 'I'm not delectable.'

'Oh, you are.' His fingers slipped beneath the soft weight of her hair. 'Delectable, and sweet, and very, very desirable.' He pulled her mouth down to his, unable to resist the urge to taste her lips again. 'So what are you going to do about it?'

'What am I going to do about it?' she echoed.

'Yeah.' He released her lips and transferred his attentions to the luscious breast that was suspended only inches above his mouth. 'You could start by telling me how you feel about me.'

'Oh, God!' Eve bent over him, cradling his face between her palms. 'You know I love you,' she exclaimed fervently. 'But even now I can't believe that you want me.'

'Believe it,' said Jake huskily, reversing their positions so he could bury his face between her breasts. 'Ever since you came to the island you've been driving me crazy. I knew I had to give you time, but, like I said before, I couldn't eat, I couldn't sleep, I couldn't think about anything but us being together.'

Eve was dazed by his urgency, and not a little shocked by the growing hardness against her hip. 'You—you want me again?' she breathed, the exhilaration of knowing she could do this to him sweeping over her.

'Constantly,' he said, his hand slipping between them to caress her. 'Oh, baby, you have no idea how much...'

Hours later, they had a midnight feast of strawberries and champagne. It was only right and proper that they should celebrate their unofficial engagement in such a way, Jake said, climbing back onto the bed with the bottle of champagne and two crystal glasses in his hands, and Eve stared at him in disbelief.

'Our unofficial *engagement*?' she said, blinking, and Jake grinned back at her.

'Well, you are going to marry me, aren't you?' he asked, and for a long while after that the champagne was forgotten.

But eventually Eve wriggled into a cross-legged position beside him. There were things she wanted to tell him, things she had to tell him, before their engagement became official and Jake couldn't back out.

'I need to tell you about my father,' she said, accepting a champagne-dipped strawberry from him and resting it against her lower lip.

'Your father?' Jake frowned, fascinated by her unknowing sensuality. 'I thought your mother didn't know who your father was?'

'Oh, she knew. My grandmother forced her to tell the truth when she was searching for me.' Eve bent her head. 'He was Cuban, you see, and Cassie hadn't wanted to tell the Fultons that in case they changed their minds.'

Jake gave a low whistle. 'No kidding. So—did you get to know him? Afterwards, I mean?'

'No. Ellie found out he'd been killed in a plane crash in Cuba just weeks after I was conceived. Cassie wasn't lying about that, at least. He didn't want to know that he'd fathered a child.'

'Oh, sweetheart.' Jake pulled her close and pressed a warm kiss to the top of her head. 'You certainly had a raw deal.'

Eve glanced up at him. 'You don't mind?'

'Why should I mind?'

'Oh, I don't know.' Eve hesitated. 'Harry seemed to think it was important that I was half Cuban.'

'Who? That idiot priest back at Falconbridge?' And, at her nod, 'Was that what upset you so much that night?'

'It was the way he said it. And the fact that he thought I was only putting him off because I was attracted to you,' said Eve honestly.

'Hey, the guy had a brain after all.'

Eve cuddled close. 'I do love you, you know.'

'I know,' said Jake smugly. 'That's why you're going to marry me and not him.'

Six months later, Eve sat with Julie Romero on the terrace at the back of the villa. It was early evening, and Julie was nursing her four-month-old daughter at her breast. Watching her, Eve wondered what it would be like to feed a baby. Well, she'd know soon enough, when their baby was born.

Not that that was going to happen any time soon. In fact, apart from Jake's immediate family—and her grandmother—they'd kept the fact that Eve was expecting a baby to themselves. At present it was barely noticeable, although Eve knew her waistline was thickening by the day.

Julie finished feeding the baby and, after adjusting the bodice of her dress, shifted the baby to her shoulder. 'Thank goodness that's over,' she said, with feeling. 'I didn't realise a baby's jaws could be so strong.'

Eve smiled. 'Here,' she said. 'Give her to me.'

'She's heavy.'

'Not that heavy,' said Eve firmly. Then, after settling the baby over her own shoulder, she said, 'What time is Mike getting back?'

'Pretty soon, I hope,' said Julie fervently. And then, realising how that might sound, she added, 'Not that I haven't appreciated you and Jake letting me stay here while he's been away. But I've missed him, you know. Even three days can seem like for ever when you're apart.'

'I know.' Eve was sympathetic, but she was also grateful that Jake had unloaded a lot of the overseas travelling onto his younger brother's shoulders. It meant they spent a lot more time together, and whenever he did travel Eve went with him.

And, as if thinking about him had attracted his attention, Jake chose that moment to come out of the house. 'Mike's just rung,' he said, his eyes going to his wife and the baby. 'He landed a few minutes ago. He's coming straight here.'

'Oh, marvellous!' Julie beamed, and Jake patted her on the shoulder before going to join his wife and baby Rachel on the glider. Julie got up. 'I'll just go and smarten myself up.'

Jake smiled at his sister-in-law as she went into the house, and then at the baby, trailing a caressing finger down Eve's bare arm. 'You know, having visitors can be rather limiting,' he murmured. 'I haven't made love with you anywhere except in our bedroom for almost a week.'

Eve dimpled. 'Is that a problem?'

'What do you think?' His lips caressed her shoulder. 'I prefer having you all to myself.'

'Well, when our baby's born—'

'—he won't care what his mother and father get up to,' said Jake firmly. 'Not for years and years.'

'And it is six months away,' agreed Eve consideringly. 'You might have got tired of making love to me by then.'

'I'll never get tired of making love to you,' asserted Jake fiercely. 'I feel as though I've been sleepwalking for most of my life. Only since I met you have I realised exactly what I was missing. We fit together. Without you I was never totally complete.'

Eve tipped her head onto his shoulder. 'That's a nice thing to say.'

'It's the truth.'

'And I'm the luckiest woman in the world.' She smiled.

'I'm so glad Ellie phoned you and told you what was going on.'

'So am I,' said Jake fervently. 'Although I didn't know if you'd agree to take the job at the school. If you hadn't, I guess I'd have had to find another reason to visit Falconbridge. Though I'd have been devastated if I'd found that your grandmother had sold the house and you weren't there any more.'

'Someone would have directed you to Adam's farm,' said Eve at once. 'But I'm glad it didn't come to that. Ellie so much enjoyed coming here for the wedding. And Adam and his family... I bet they're still talking about travelling in a private plane.'

Jake looked sheepish. 'Yeah, I guess Adam and I got off on the wrong foot, didn't we?'

'Well, neither of you was exactly friendly towards the other.'

'You know why?' Jake grimaced. 'I thought he was another friend of yours. And poor old Adam thought I was another of Cassie's hangers-on.'

Eve pulled a face now. 'She won't like it when she hears she's going to be a grandmother.'

'Like I care what that woman thinks.'

'Well, she did make an effort and send us a wedding present,' said Eve charitably. 'And I'm so happy, Jake. I can't forget that without her we'd never have met.'

Jake sighed. 'Okay. But I can't forget the way she treated you when you were a baby. You can ask me to forgive her, but I'll never forget.'

Nor would she, thought Eve, as Jake put his arm about her. She probed the small mound at her waist with a gentle hand. Her baby would be loved, not just by her and Jake, but by all his family. The way a baby should be, she thought, burying her face in the warm hollow of Jake's neck.

HARLEQUIN *Presents*

We're delighted to announce that

A Mediterranean Marriage

is taking place—and you are invited!

Imagine blue skies, an azure sea, a beautiful landscape and the hot sun. What a perfect place to get married! But although all ends well for these couples, their route to happiness is filled with emotion and passion.

Follow their journey in the latest book from this miniseries.

In **THE GREEK'S CHOSEN WIFE**, Prudence Demarkis will consummate her marriage to tycoon Nikolos Angelis. She wants a baby, he wants a wife; together they will learn to make a marriage.

Get your copy today!

THE GREEK'S CHOSEN WIFE is on sale March 2006, wherever books are sold.

www.eHarlequin.com

HPAMMU306

uNcut

Even more passion for your reading pleasure!

Escape into a world of passion and romance!

You'll find the drama, the emotion, the international settings and happy endings that you love in Presents. But we've turned up the thermostat a little, so that the relationships really sizzle…. Careful, they're almost too hot to handle!

Check out the first book in this brand-new miniseries….

Cameron Knight is on a dangerous mission when he rescues Leanna.

THE DESERT VIRGIN,
by Sandra Marton

on sale this March.

"The Desert Virgin has it all from thrills to danger to romance to passion."
—Shannon Short, *Romantic Times BOOKclub* reviewer

Look out for two more thrilling Knight Brothers stories, coming in May and July!

www.eHarlequin.com

HPUC0306

If you enjoyed what you just read,
then we've got an offer you can't resist!

Take 2 bestselling love stories FREE!

Plus get a FREE surprise gift!

Clip this page and mail it to Harlequin Reader Service®

IN U.S.A.	IN CANADA
3010 Walden Ave.	P.O. Box 609
P.O. Box 1867	Fort Erie, Ontario
Buffalo, N.Y. 14240-1867	L2A 5X3

YES! Please send me 2 free Harlequin Presents® novels and my free surprise gift. After receiving them, if I don't wish to receive anymore, I can return the shipping statement marked cancel. If I don't cancel, I will receive 6 brand-new novels every month, before they're available in stores! In the U.S.A., bill me at the bargain price of $3.80 plus 25¢ shipping & handling per book and applicable sales tax, if any*. In Canada, bill me at the bargain price of $4.47 plus 25¢ shipping & handling per book and applicable taxes**. That's the complete price and a savings of at least 10% off the cover prices—what a great deal! I understand that accepting the 2 free books and gift places me under no obligation ever to buy any books. I can always return a shipment and cancel at any time. Even if I never buy another book from Harlequin, the 2 free books and gift are mine to keep forever.

106 HDN DZ7Y
306 HDN DZ7Z

Name	(PLEASE PRINT)	
Address	Apt.#	
City	State/Prov.	Zip/Postal Code

Not valid to current Harlequin Presents® subscribers.

Want to try two free books from another series?
Call 1-800-873-8635 or visit www.morefreebooks.com.

* Terms and prices subject to change without notice. Sales tax applicable in N.Y.
** Canadian residents will be charged applicable provincial taxes and GST.
  All orders subject to approval. Offer limited to one per household.
  ® are registered trademarks owned and used by the trademark owner and or its licensee.

PRES04R   ©2004 Harlequin Enterprises Limited

e◆HARLEQUIN.com

The Ultimate Destination for Women's Fiction

Becoming an eHarlequin.com member is easy, fun and **FREE!** Join today to enjoy great benefits:

- **Super savings** on all our books, including members-only discounts and offers!

- Enjoy **exclusive online reads**—FREE!

- Info, tips and **expert advice** on writing your own romance novel.

- FREE romance **newsletters,** customized by you!

- Find out the latest on your **favorite authors.**

- Enter to win exciting **contests and promotions!**

- Chat with other members in our **community message boards!**

To become a member, visit www.eHarlequin.com today!

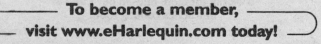

INTMEMB04R

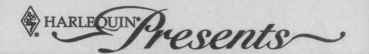

Men who can't be tamed... Or so they think!

If you love strong, commanding men, you'll love
this brand-new miniseries.

Meet the hard-edged, handsome, rich and rakish man
who breaks the rules to get exactly what he wants.
He's ruthless!

THE BILLIONAIRE BOSS'S FORBIDDEN MISTRESS

by Miranda Lee

In Miranda Lee's latest book, Jason Pollock expects
his beautiful new receptionist to fall at his feet—and is
surprised to find she's more of a challenge
than he thought....

THE BILLIONAIRE BOSS'S FORBIDDEN MISTRESS
On sale March 2006.

Look out for more titles in our *Ruthless*
miniseries coming soon!

www.eHarlequin.com
HPRUTH0306